A Turkish Affair

Matilda Voss

A Turkish Affair

On the brink of divorce, and with her fiftieth birthday just around the corner, Zoe's life is far from perfect. Out of the blue, she receives a card from an ex-lover from over twenty six years ago which completely turns her world upside down and has her questioning her life. She reminisces on how they first met in 1980 when she was backpacking through Greece and struggles with her decision to be reunited with him again in Turkey in 2007. Together they travel to Cappadocia for a six day sojourn and to see if there could possibly be any future in their relationship.

'In my heart of hearts I desperately wanted this. Murat made me feel alive and I knew that a few days together would be therapeutic and liberating. For years now there had been no intimacy in my marriage and the thought of being touched and loved by a man again sent shivers down my spine.'

PART ONE

How it all began

2006

Chapter One

"Sometimes the slightest things change the directions of our lives, the merest breath of a circumstance, a random moment that connects like a meteorite striking the earth. Lives have swivelled and changed direction on the strength on a chance remark." Bryce Courtney.

I didn't know it at the time but a meteorite *was heading my way, blazing and bright. I could never have foreseen the power* of its impact. In retrospect, I can categorically pinpoint the day and the catalyst that was to trigger a chain of events and chance happenings that would utterly change the direction of my life and take me half way around the world.

It was a hot and steamy December afternoon in rural New South Wales, Australia. I was alerted to the soft muffled purring of the small postie bike as it waited at our welcoming tree whilst the letters were sorted and shoved into the old rusty milk can, come letter box. He always came at about this time and I always enjoyed the stroll out through my garden, through the farm gate and out onto the road where our letterbox was attached to this magnificent eucalyptus tree that was playing host to a strangler fig. Over the past ten years or so, we watched as the strangler fig slowly but surely sent out new feelers that wrapped themselves around the trunk of this hospitable blue gum.

"Thanks Gary", I called with a wave but he was already on his way up the road to our neighbour's house.

Christmas cards continued to arrive and I felt a little guilty as I had decided to refrain from sending any this year. It seemed so pointless and I wasn't in a very Christmassy mood anyway. A Christmas card from the dentist and one from the accountant, it seems Christmas is a perfect opportunity to advertise one's business. Then there were the shopping catalogues with pretty pictures of children playing around the Christmas tree and the Christmas feast. For God sakes, this is Australia. It is way too hot for a traditional Christmas feast and most people spend the day at the beach.

One card stood out. It was in a large oversized envelop and it was my mum's shaky handwriting. We had just talked a few days ago and she knew I didn't want any Christmas cards.

I sat down on the cane chair on my verandah sorting through the mail and kept this one for last. The air was heavy and I could feel a storm was brewing. The scent of the citrus was thick and the sound of insects buzzing in the grevillea blossoms was music to my ears. A long trail of ants made their way across the pavers, carrying their prey to their nest and preparing for the impending storm.

I loved observing the pre-storm activities of our resident animals and insects. Our friendly lorikeets dropped by for an afternoon snack on the bird feeder. I decided to get myself a chardonnay, take a seat out on the deck and have a look through the Christmas brochures and see what my mum had sent me. Matt would be home from school soon.

I was intrigued as to what she had sent and why. I examined it carefully and it was sent just two days before. I stuck my finger into the top corner and gently prized the envelope open. Inside was another envelope. This envelope was blue and bore a stamp and postmark from Turkey. It was addressed to Zoe Reynolds, my maiden name and sent to my mother's address. My heart skipped a beat when I turned it over and read the name of the sender. I needed that chardonnay now and greedily gulped from the glass. My mind was doing backflips. What could this mean? What had he sent me? Gosh, how long had it been?

It was a card, a water colour painting of a beach scene with children playing in the sand. Inside was a simple message; 'My dear Zoe, are you still alive? I have thought about you every day since we were last together. Love always, Murat.'

Wow, I tried to think about when we were last together. Must be nearly thirty years ago, I calculated, a life time ago. My mind was trying to recall our last days together. I was totally lost in thought when the school bus's squeaky brakes outside our gate brought me back to the present moment and Matt came sauntering down the path.

"Hiya," he said.

"How was your day, darling?" I enquired, trying to steady my voice.

"Good, got lots of homework. Got a maths test on Friday. I'm starving, what's for dinner?"

Matt was finishing up his last year of junior high school. Exams and assignments were almost overwhelming and the pressure from his school to excel was at times too much, but he handled it all very well. We both knew that the next two years, the final senior years and preparing for the university entrance exams would be worse.

"There's some freshly baked blueberry muffins on the kitchen counter and I think we'll do a barbecue for dinner. What do you think?" I asked.

"Sounds good to me," he replied. "Might have a quick jump in the pool before the storm. It's so hot today."

We could hear the distant rumbling as the storm was approaching. Matt took to the pool for a quick cool down and I went and got all the washing off the line.

It was just me and Matt at home now. Steve had moved out and was working interstate and Ben, my eldest was at university in Sydney. Matt and I, we made a great team. After the last few years, I felt I could finally breathe. The decision for Steve to move out was the best decision ever. We needed to face the facts that our marriage just wasn't working anymore. It wasn't good for either of us. And with all our arguing and bickering, we hadn't been setting the best example for the boys. Life was just so much more relaxed now that Steve didn't live at home.

He came home for a weekend every couple of months and we both tried to just get through it. We would go out for dinner and act as a normal family but we both knew it was over. I always felt this immense sense of relief as his car pulled out of the driveway to return to his work. In fact, the longer I was alone, the stronger I felt and the more certain that I wanted a divorce. But at the moment, my first and most important priority was to get Matt through his final years of school as easily and stress-free as possible.

We could hear the distant thunder. It was getting closer.

"Time to go take a shower, Matt. That storm is almost upon us," I called.

I busied myself with folding the washing, and marinating some chicken for the barbecue, but the card was on mind. Crazy, that it should come now.

Just last week, Cheryl and I had been for our weekly lunch date and had been reminiscing about past loves and I had actually spoken his name. How's that for a coincidence? Every week Cheryl and I walk the beautiful headland trail and take in the sea breeze and all those energising negative ions. I always looked forward to it. After walking the six or so kilometres, we would treat ourselves to a relaxing lunch down at the beach kiosk. We would spend the rest of the afternoon chatting and gossiping until it was time to pick up the kids from school.

This week, for some reason, the conversation turned to boyfriends and all the loves we had in our earlier years. Usually we discussed my marriage situation. Cheryl was a much appreciated confidante. I could tell her everything and anything, she never judged, always listened and always gave very sound advice. Steve and I hadn't been content for a long time now. We had definitely grown apart and I couldn't see any way to fix it. I didn't want to fix it. We had nothing in common anymore. He had his work and that was his life. My interests didn't interest him in the least and I wasn't particularly interested in roads and roundabouts either. I don't think he even saw me anymore. We had just drifted apart and I knew that when Matt was off to university, I would be off too.

During this week's lunch date Cheryl had talked about her first love, who incidentally turned out to be the man she married and they were still very much in love. I told her about my first love when I had just left school but we were too young and anyway, I wanted to travel before getting serious with anyone. And travel is what I did; my epic European adventure in my twenties. Of course, during my travels I had had the odd holiday romance. Where had that Zoe gone, the adventurous Zoe, the Zoe that laughed and embraced all that life had to offer, fun Zoe? Where was she now? I certainly didn't feel like fun Zoe anymore.

Wait till I tell Cheryl about the card from Murat. What would she say? She would see how coincidental it was, having just talked about him and now receiving a card from him, especially since I probably hadn't uttered his name in almost thirty years.

"These muffins are yum," exclaimed Matt and breaking my moments of nostalgia and thought.

"Well don't eat too many, as we'll make dinner in an hour or so." I said "You can barbecue the chicken and I'll make a big salad and how about ice-cream for dessert?"

"Sounds good," said Matt as he came over to kiss me on the forehead.

He was almost six foot tall and definitely the man of the house now. I depended on him to help with the lawns, clean the pool and all the other little home duties that needed to be done. He even got up on the roof and cleaned the gutters and chopped down all the overhanging branches. I constantly felt blessed to have two incredible boys. Ben would help as much as he could too, when he came home from university. I was looking forward to him being home for Christmas. Seeing the boys together, jamming in the garage and just hanging out like old times gave me a lot of joy. If I'd done anything phenomenal in this life, it was giving birth to these two amazing human beings. At least something wonderful had come out of this marriage.

"Who's that from?" remarked Matt, pointing to the card now sitting on the kitchen bench.

"An old friend," I replied, "Someone from my travelling days, many moons ago."

****

8

That night after dinner, when Matt was in his room studying, I began searching through my old photo albums. I knew I had some photos of him. Gosh, I hadn't looked at these albums for decades. They were hidden away under all the baby albums at the bottom of the cupboard and hadn't seen the light of day for quite a while. It was funny to see the young me, fresh faced and full of life. And there he was, a photo of him down on the beach, young, invincible, a different lifetime ago. I sank to the floor, memories came flooding back. Why after all these years has he resurfaced into my life?

As I slowly turned the pages of my photo albums, each photo triggered a memory. There was a picture of my travel companion Lynn and me in our matching anoraks, same anorak different colours. Lynn sported the red one and me in the blue. We also went shopping for back packs. We would leave our suitcases in London and travel with just a pack on our backs. Intrepid travellers we would be. Again, Lynn had a red pack and mine was blue. Looking at the photo now, I couldn't imagine how we carried those things. Large and cumbersome with an external metal frame, they didn't look anywhere as comfy as the ones you see these days. But Lynn and I looked pretty pleased with ourselves as we posed for these photos.

"What ya doin'?" Matt's question brought me back to the present moment.

"I'm just looking at my old photo albums, my travels through Europe in the early eighties." I replied.

"Here, this is a photo of the guy from whom I received the card from today. His name is Murat," I said as I handed an old loose photo to Matt.

It was Murat sitting bare chested at a taverna on the beach, glass of retsina in hand and that radiant smile of his.

Matt looked through the album and sniggered at the photos of the younger version of his mum. I felt slightly proud of my travels.

"Yes Matt, I had a life before you kids came along. I travelled a lot and have some brilliant memories."

Matt pointed to a photo of Murat playing an electric guitar up on a large stage.

"Ah, he plays guitar." Matt seemed impressed. He was a very keen guitarist himself and anything to do with guitars rocked.

"Yes, that photo was taken before I met him. He was playing in a band at the wedding party of his cousin, if I remember rightly." I began to recall the day he gave that photo out of his wallet. Maybe that was our last day together.

Together we looked through the albums and I enjoyed sharing this chapter of my life with Matt. It seemed so long ago and so far away. Where had all the years gone? Now here I was about to turn fifty and out of the blue comes this short message that has totally transported me back to the eighties, to a time of freedom and spontaneity, party time, no responsibilities, just a desire to live every moment of life to its fullest.

"Wow, you look so young, mum," commented Matt. "Where's dad?"

"That was a few years before I met your dad, darling," I smiled. "Those were my adventure years."

1980

Chapter Two

I had been working in an office for a health insurance company. I had worked there for four years already. After leaving school I had done a year at university but when this job came along, I dropped out. It seemed an excellent idea at the time. It was a decent job and paid well but the nine to five routine was becoming tedious and I longed for change and some excitement. Also, I wasn't getting on well with my mother, and I just wanted to escape into the world. I knew there was a big wide world out there calling me to all those exotic places I had read about and studied at school.

It had been an impulsive decision one lunch time and I bought myself a one way flight ticket to London. Well, I remember going into the travel agents office to enquire about the price and then the woman behind the desk asked, "Shall I book it?" and being taken totally by surprise, I just answered "Yes". It cost me around five hundred dollars, my biggest purchase to date.

I had run back to work feeling dizzy with excitement and also slightly scared at what I had just done. What had I just done? As much as it was a big decision and clearly an impulsive one, it had felt right. I didn't know how I was going to tell my mother and in fact, I hadn't told her until a couple of weeks before my departure. I just knew it would cause a problem and she'd go off at me about being reckless, and she did.

But the weeks rolled by and in February 1980 I said goodbye to my friends, work buddies, my mother and brother and boarded the plane for London. It was an exhilarating feeling, the feeling of freedom and not knowing what was ahead of me. I had no real plans and if it didn't work out, I could always come home. I needed to at least give it a go. I felt that life had more to offer me than the mundane routine that I was living at the moment and I had saved my money for a while now. I'd get a job in London. Aussies had an excellent reputation for their work ethic and it wouldn't be a problem. It would all work out. I was young, optimistic and yes, maybe slightly reckless, but the sense of adventure was sweeping me along.

As the plane touched down in Heathrow I knew that a new chapter of my life was beginning. I had organised my first week's stay in London at an establishment in Bayswater called the Colonial Club; a very corny name, I know. It was basically a youth hostel for young travellers, mostly Australians. I was in a dorm with three other girls and it turned out to be so much fun. That's how I met Lynn.

Lynn and I hit it off instantly. She had just arrived from Perth with as many plans as I had. We both had no idea what our next step would be, but had faith that something would come along to help us decide our path. For us, every day was now an adventure. Coming from Australia in the eighties, of course we were naïve and innocent. Australia was so cut off from the rest of the world in those pre-internet days. Now, here we were surrounded by a hugely multi-cultural crowd, a range of different accents and the Cockney one, in particular, being music to our ears. It was brilliant. London was exhilarating and definitely eye opening for two young Aussie gals.

Together we explored this remarkable city and all its sights and sounds. At the end of a day's sightseeing, we enjoyed the socialising downstairs in the Colonial Club bar where the beer was cheap, if not warm but the music was loud and really rocking. The infamous 'Down Under Bar' was only a block away and another fun place to hang out. AC/DC rocked the roof and we just danced and drank way too much beer but we were young and we were in London. It was an incredible time.

One night during those first exciting weeks in London, we met two Greek guys who were working down in the Colonial Club bar. These guys told us all about their country and it sounded amazing. They told us how the weather was much better there than in England. They painted a magical picture and their photos and stories were intoxicating.

Greece had definitely been one of the countries I had wanted to visit. My ancient history studies had left a deep impression in my heart and I knew I had to see all the places that I had read about. Our Greek friends had sown the seeds and Lynn and I couldn't stop thinking about Greece. We saw it as the sign that we had been waiting for. It gave us a direction for our first travels. This would be our first big adventure. The decision was made, we would go to Greece.

Now, we needed to arrange how we would travel to Greece. We were budget minded back packers living on a shoe string and so the obvious choice was the bus, which had been recommended to us. It was called the Magic Bus and cost something like twenty pounds for a three night bus trip from London to Athens. Oh, we were so naïve and so unprepared. What were we thinking?

And so, on a cold and rainy London late afternoon in April, we left the safety and comfort of our hostel and boarded the bus, hearts full of excitement and joy at the prospect of travelling to Greece.

2006

Chapter Three

"Hey, just got your message," exclaimed Cheryl on the phone. "That's so crazy that we just talked about him the other day and then you get this card. What did he say?"

"Not much, just that he thinks of me always. He wonders if I'm still alive," I chuckled.

"And did he leave an address or someway that you can contact him?"

"Yes. Just his email and messenger address," I replied.

"What? Well, did you go online and contact him?" she queried.

"No, why would I? I mean what could he want? I'm a married woman, after all. Don't think it would be proper to be chatting to an old boyfriend. Do you?" I replied.

"Well, yes. Why not? You can block him if there's a problem and anyway, you are on the brink of divorce. It's not like you are being unfaithful. You don't even live together anymore," she retorted.

"Hmm, I guess you are right, but it still feels wrong. I don't know. What would we talk about? I mean, Cheryl, it's been like twenty six years since I last saw him. We were young and now we're not. He would be in his fifties already and I'm nearly there."

"That means you would have so much to talk about. It would be fun to chat and see what each other has been up to. You never know what could come from this. And besides Zoe, he is on the other side of the planet, so I think you'll be safe," she chortled.

"Well okay, but Steve's coming home for Christmas so I'll need to wait till after he's gone back to work before I can make contact with him."

"For Christ's sake Zoe, it's still two weeks till Christmas. Put in his Messenger address now and let me know what happens. This is so exciting," she replied. "I'll be waiting for your call and all the news."

I hung up the phone and did a little skip around the kitchen. Okay, maybe she was right. Maybe I should contact him; after all, a little chat with an old friend couldn't hurt. I wondered if he had married, if he had any children. What work was he doing now? What had

18

happened since last time I'd seen him? There were many questions.

The next morning, after Matt had left for school, I turned on the computer and waited for it to warm up and connect to the internet. I had opened my Messenger account and entered his address. It seemed he was online. I hadn't even thought about any time differences but he was online anyway. Within minutes I heard the familiar ping and up popped his message; 'Hello, Zoe?'

1980

Chapter Four

The bus we boarded in London was a modern comfortable coach. This wasn't going to be too bad and the ticket price was certainly appealing. That first night we celebrated the beginning of our journey with a meal and a wine on board the Dover ferry as our bus crossed over the English Channel to the French port of Calais. So far, these first few hours of our trip had been perfect.

As our coach slowly pulled off the ferry, we watched out of our window at all the lights and activity at the Calais Port. We had arrived in France. We looked at each other and our grins beamed from ear to ear. "We're in France," we both exclaimed with a screech.

As our bus drove out of the port, we passed long queues of cars and buses waiting to embark on their journey back to Dover. We were on our way and though it was now the early hours of the morning, our enthusiasm fuelled us and we eagerly watched out of the window until all the hustle and bustle of the port was behind us.

Before not too long, our coach pulled into a parkway and we were all instructed off our lovely, warm and comfortable coach. We gathered our packs from the underneath luggage storage and were ushered onto another bus. Greek hieroglyphics adorned the side of this rattily old bus that was to be our home for the next three days. As we all boarded, it became apparent that there would not be enough seats and so people were forced to fit three to a seat and some chose to sit in the aisle. The bus was filled to overcapacity and no one was smiling now. The protests began but what could anyone do.

As the engine started firing, our 'new' bus heaved into action, spluttering and coughing. Any complaints from our fellow passengers were soon drowned out by the loud and lively sounds of Greek music that blared from the loudspeakers. Lynn and I looked at each other. We were no longer grinning. We realised that a long few days were ahead of us.

We soon began chatting to the two guys in the seat in front of us. They were British, John and Simon, both recently graduated and on a quest to explore the Peloponnesus of Greece. They had been to Greece before and had even done the Magic Bus before. They laughed at our horror and discomfort.

"Hey, at least you have got a seat. And this is the cheapest way to get to Athens. Don't worry it will be over before you know it, so just suck it up and enjoy the ride," said John with a grin as he offered us a biscuit.

"Do we stop for toilet breaks and meal breaks?" I asked.

"Maybe, if we're lucky," said John, obviously enjoying our discomfort. "Don't worry, we'll look after you. We've got heaps of snacks."

Lynn and I hadn't really counted on this and had only bought a few packs of chips and water, not enough for three days. At the moment we were still satisfied from our feast upon the ferry, but that wouldn't sustain us the entire trip. Well at least we had each other and now we had two new friends, who besides laughing at our naivety, did seem like two decent guys who would look after us.

The music bellowed and the bus filled with the cigarette smoke of our drivers. We heard the clinking of bottles only to discover to our horror that our driver was swigging from a bottle of Johnny Walker.

We drove on through the night and always welcomed the day. Dirty road house restaurants and border checks punctuated our days and eventually we arrived in Greece and couldn't have been more grateful and relieved to have arrived in Athens alive. The Magic Bus had got us there. Perhaps that's how it got its name.

Athens welcomed us with icy cold and driving rain and before long we and our packs were drenched. We had decided to stick with John and Simon until we got our bearings, and we followed them to a budget hotel and checked into a room for four. A shower and an afternoon nap were first and foremost on everyone's mind. With no shower or change of clothes in three days, we definitely had that wet stray dog smell. That first shower was heaven and the bed was the most comfortable bed in the world. We had made it. We were in Greece.

The four of us slept like logs and it was early evening when hunger pains woke us and our next priority was food. We felt we deserved a feast, a Greek feast and John knew exactly the place to go for a satisfying and cheap meal.

We followed him into a Greek taverna and were instantly engulfed by the warmth and aroma from the kitchen. The table was laid, a basket of warm crusty bread and a bottle of the local retsina first to arrive. This was followed by the colourful and flavoursome Greek salad, pieces of tomatoes, sliced cucumbers, red onions, feta cheese, and large Kalamata olives tossed in an aromatic olive oil with oregano and a pinch of salt. I couldn't resist picking an olive from the top of the plate.

We were invited into the kitchen to view and select more food. Everything looked so fresh and inviting but we went with the moussaka, layers of eggplant and meat topped off with a creamy béchamel sauce, and the grilled skewers of lamb known as souvlaki.

That first evening in Athens was perfect, but we were still so very tired, and so an early night was needed. The next day John and Simon were heading down to the Peloponnesus to explore the ancient sites of Mycenae, Epidaurus and Argos. Lynn and I had plenty to explore in Athens. We were really grateful to the guys and thankful for their friendship. We decided to try to meet up again a few days later at a town down on the Peloponnesus called Nafplio. Sounded like a fun idea and we certainly enjoyed their company.

That morning Lynn and I enjoyed our first Greek breakfast of fresh bread, homemade butter and honey and of course, coffee. The guys had left early but we were in no rush. We were content to relax, write up our diaries and browse through the guidebook, whilst enjoying another coffee. We were free. We had no responsibilities and no deadlines, only a thirst for adventure.

Over the next few days we explored the sights of Athens from the majestic Acropolis and the Parthenon to Syntagma Square and the Changing of the Guards. We wandered the Plaka and enjoyed the arrival of some spring weather, sitting out at the terraces whilst relishing the delectable Greek food. It was like a dream come true. Everything I'd read about in my Ancient History class was now at my fingertips.

A few days later we boarded the bus for Nafplio with the hope that we would be able to locate the guys. They had given us the name of a youth hostel where they would be staying for a while.

Chapter Five

Arriving in Nafplio, the sky was a sheet of brilliant blue and the sea was sparkling. We swung our packs on to our backs and wandered down along the cobbled lanes to the town centre. A massive fortress crowned the hill that overlooked the town and its picturesque fishing port. Pretty tavernas and outdoor cafés beckoned us but we needed to find a hotel first. The thought of sleeping in a dormitory in a youth hostel didn't appeal to either Lynn or me. We preferred a hotel room and it didn't take us long to find one and get settled in. We decided on a little chill time and would wait till later before going in search of the guys.

****

Strolling along the cobbled lanes down towards the port, we soon stumbled upon the youth hostel and just as we were entering the foyer, there was Simon.

"Hey, you came. That's great. We're in here," he said as he led us down the hall to their dormitory.

John jumped up off his bunk when he saw us.

"Surprise," Lynn and I called.

"You found us."

We were all together again. It felt good. Hugging and kissing like long lost friends who had all survived something memorable together. The Magic Bus ordeal would always be the common bond we shared and the subject of many of our conversations.

"So," said John, "how did you guys like Athens?"

"It was awesome," I answered. "We had a really cool time seeing the sights and sampling the food. We kept going back to the same place you took us. Their food was so fresh and tasty and they were always very kind to us."

The conversation flowed and we had so much to catch up on. It had only been a few days but we had so many stories to tell and experiences to share.

"How funny is the Changing of the Guards?" I said. "The guys in their little white dresses and pompom shoes."

"Their goose stepping was pretty weird to watch," added Lynn.

"Did you get up to the Temple of the Greek God Zeus?" asked John

"Yes, I think we saw all the main sights. We sure did walk a lot and everything is on a hill. We still can't believe we're here, in Greece," we both nodded. "We even met some nice Greek boys," I joked. We had met a couple of Greek guys one evening and enjoyed a couple of drinks with them.

"Hey, let's go to this neat little taverna on the beach that we discovered," suggested John. "The food is fresh and cheap. They might even have live music tonight," he added, "and we can have a few drinks before dinner."

We all agreed that that was a good idea. Lynn and I were quite hungry and if we moved quickly we might get to see the sun set over the bay. The guys grabbed their jackets and just as we were leaving, John turned a moment and hesitated.

"Listen girls, we met this guy here and he came with us on our trip to Mycenae. He's really cool, he's Turkish and his name is Murat. His English isn't that good but it's okay. Do you mind if we invite him to join us?" asked John.

Lynn and I looked at each other, and together we replied, "Sure, the more the merrier."

"Okay, cheers, one minute. I'll go get him. You guys go ahead and we'll be there shortly," said John.

Together we followed Simon, chattering all the way, down to the taverna by the sea. The scent of garlic and grilled seafood filled the air and our stomachs were growling by now. We took a table near the sea front, blue and white checkered table clothes and wooden chairs, and together we watched as the sun slowly sank into the horizon.

It wasn't too long till our meditation was broken and a waiter joined us with a basket of crusty bread and a bottle of chilled water. He gave us the menus and invited us inside to see the kitchen if we wished. We asked for a bottle of retsina and five glasses to start and would wait for the others before we ordered but I couldn't help myself from snacking on a piece of bread from the basket.

Sitting back, enjoying the sound of the lapping waves and the iridescent pink sky, we soon heard John and his new friend approaching.

"Hello. This is Murat," he said as he then proceeded to introduce each of us and we all shook hands.

I smiled. I took a deep breath. I'm sure my heart had just skipped a beat. I couldn't take my eyes off our new friend, this handsome stranger who had joined us for dinner. He smiled back at me and I'm sure I felt an electric shock. I definitely felt my stomach flutter.

29

I turned to Lynn. "What do you think?" I whispered. "Isn't he gorgeous?"

My attraction was instant. Murat had shoulder length wavy golden brown hair, a short beard and moustache, deep brown eyes and perfect olive skin. He had a rather hippie appearance, dressed in loose linen pants and a grandpa collared shirt. He wore various leather straps and beaded necklaces around his neck and wrists. He seemed intense and somewhat reserved. I was captivated.

I tried to act normal and join in the conversation but I couldn't take my eyes off Murat; his smile, his eyes. His every movement and mannerism intrigued me. I had to force myself to stop staring and hope to God he hadn't noticed.

The retsina began to flow, mouth-watering dishes covered our table and the evening was off to a perfect start. We shared our stories about Athens and listened intently to the guy's stories of their day exploring the archaeological site of the ancient city of Mycenae. Of course, our conversation turned once more to our experience on the Magic Bus and how we had risked our lives in the hands of the chain smoking and whiskey drinking Greek drivers. We explained to Murat about the intense and very scary border checks where we often had to hand over our backpacks and allow the very intimidating guards to rummage through our belongings. One night, one of our fellow passengers was even taken away and we had all feared the worst. We waited and waited and luckily a couple of hours later he was returned to us, safe and sound with a great travel tale to tell.

I for one, was very interested to hear about Murat; a Turkish man in Greece.

"What brought you to Greece, Murat?" I asked

His voice was soft and he wasn't confident speaking English, but he tried to answer.

"I come Rize, Black Sea," he replied. "I must Turkey leave. Not soldier want."

John took it upon himself to fully explain for Murat.

"In Turkey, military service is compulsory. If you don't do your military service which can be up to eighteen months, you will go to prison and I can't imagine a Turkish prison being any fun," John explained. "Therefore, Murat escaped to Greece. He has had to leave his family and the country he loves, but he is a pacifist and doesn't want to be a soldier. His country is at war with a group of people called the Kurds that live in northern Iraq and south eastern Turkey and he doesn't believe in this war. Now he is looking to find work. He's done some work on the fishing boats here."

Lynn and I were intrigued. He was a fugitive, on the run from his own country. If he returned home, he would surely go to prison. A surge of compassion flooded my being and I was even more captivated by our new friend.

Murat nodded as John explained his predicament.

"I happy new friends have," he said as we all raised our glasses and toasted our new friendships.

"To finding work and happy days," we cheered.

The evening continued into the morning hours. From inside the restaurant we could hear the sound of the bouzouki and the loud cheers and clapping hands of the patrons, but outside on the terrace we enjoyed a clear starlit night and the lights of the fishing boats out to sea.

As much as I was charmed by our new friend Murat, I could feel his gaze upon me also and we managed to sneak an occasional smile to each other. I wasn't imagining it. There was definitely a connection. I wanted to know more about him, about his life in Turkey, his family, his passions and pastimes.

The clear night sky heralded another sunny day down on the Peloponnesus and so we all agreed on a picnic day at one of the nearby coves. If we went home now we could get a few decent hours of sleep and meet again around midday at the hostel.

After saying our goodbyes, hugs and kisses, Lynn and I wearily wandered the cobbled streets home and straight to bed. We had drunk a little too much retsina perhaps.

Barely a word was spoken about our evening and our new friend, but I knew that she had noticed something going on and we would inevitable talk about Murat tomorrow.

2006

Chapter Six

"Well, did you contact him? What did he say?" probed Cheryl. "Was it okay?"

"Yes, I think it was. It felt a little bit strange at first, this person from the past, a friend and yet a stranger. I could tell that his English is much better now. It wasn't too long till we both relaxed and then it just seemed like old times. Certainly didn't seem like twenty six years have passed. How crazy is that?" I answered.

I could see the excitement in Cheryl's face. She was smiling from ear to ear and eager to hear more.

"Come on, what else did he say? Did you ask him why he sent you that card? Why now? Come on, Zoe," she encouraged.

"Well after our initial greetings and simple chit chat, we got down to the more serious stuff. We probably chatted for well over an hour. He is married with two sons, similar ages actually as Ben and Matt. He is separated, like me. His wife threw him out of their apartment and he is now living with his sister and niece," I explained.

"Wow," exclaimed Cheryl. "Where do they live? Istanbul?"

"Yes. He is now living in Istanbul but his wife and kids live in another city. I forget the name. Not far away."

"What does he do? I mean does he work?" asked Cheryl

"Cheryl…. so many questions. Yes, of course, he works. I don't know the correct name of his job, but he is like a traffic controller for all the boats that pass through the Bosphorus. Mostly they are cargo ships carrying produce through to the Black Sea and back. He monitors their movements and guides them along so as to avoid any collisions," I explained. "Apparently, the traffic on the Bosphorus is pretty chaotic these days. He said that there are over fifty thousand vessels a year, as well as the local ferry boats zigzagging from one side to the other, so it's very easy for a collision to occur."

"Wow, must be quite a stressful job but very interesting," said Cheryl.

"Yes. Apparently, earlier this year there was a collision between a Ukrainian cargo vessel and a local ferryboat", I continued. "No deaths but lots of people were injured. He has a huge amount of responsibility."

"Sure," agreed Cheryl. "I'd love to see Istanbul one day."

"And he has to speak lots of different languages, so that he can communicate with the ships' captains," I added.

"Really?" exclaimed Cheryl. "So his English is good then?"

"Seems to be," I replied.

"And what is wrong with his marriage? Why did they separate?" she continued.

"I didn't ask that. We aren't at that level of conversation yet," I replied. "I mean we just started chatting. I didn't tell him too much about myself either. Just that I'm married and have two wonderful sons and that my husband is working in another city."

"So you didn't tell him that you are separated too?"

"No."

We enjoyed our lunch date and continued our conversation about Murat. Of course, he would be the hot topic for quite a while now. Meanwhile, I was still a married woman and didn't feel as comfortable about it all, as Cheryl did. As she put it, I am already separated and as I've said many times, there seems no way for any reconciliation with Steve. We have grown too far apart now and since I've been living alone with Matt, I've enjoyed the peace and quiet. By my own admission, I had said that I wanted a divorce. After all, I had been miserable for a few years now. I just wanted to wait till Matt finished school.

Since Steve had moved out it had been a lot more peaceful at home. Sure, we still managed the odd disagreement on the phone, but in general we were a lot kinder to each other since we were apart. Matt and I were a dream team. Our life now was a lot more relaxed. Matt was an awesome help around the house. I enjoyed the gardening and together we had the place looking in tip top shape. Steve certainly couldn't say that we couldn't cope without him. We coped better than ever. And probably he was happier alone too. Arguing and constant bickering is such a stress and not healthy for either of us.

"So when's your next chat session with Murat?" enquired Cheryl.

"I'm not sure. He works shift work so it could be any time. He said that the time difference between Turkey and Australia isn't a problem because he works all hours," I replied. "We've only chatted that once. I'll just wait till he contacts me again. But you know that Steve will be home for Christmas and I can't really chat with Murat then, so I might stay offline till after Steve leaves."

Funny, I thought to myself. All the wonderful friendships I had lost because we couldn't keep in touch. In the eighties we didn't have the internet. We didn't have mobile phones. We didn't have Messenger or Facebook. Phone calls were very expensive. The only way to stay in touch back then was by letter writing and that usually ran its course. The kids today have it so easy.

"Did you ask him why he contacted you now, after more than twenty six years? I mean that seems strange to me," said Cheryl.

"Yes, I agree. It is a bit random. He calls it fate. Apparently, when he was moving out of the family home and packing up his stuff, a piece of paper with my address fell out of one of his books. I can actually remember writing my mum's address for him. I tore a page out of my diary. He was just lucky that my mum has lived in that same house for over thirty years."

"Wow, that is very lucky," said Cheryl. "After all these years, and over so many miles away, he found you. That's incredible." She was shaking her head in wonder.

"Not to mention that by chance he finds the little piece of paper with your address on it and your mum still lives in that house," she added. "I think he's right. That is fate."

"I guess so. Life is like that at times," I pondered.

"Zoe, I don't believe in coincidences. You know that. I mean, he is separated, you are separated. This could be the beginning of something special."

"Oh, I don't think so," I replied. "As you said, he is just an old friend making contact when he came across my address. A blast from the past. Come on, we have all lost friendships from those pre-internet days, and if the opportunity arose, I'm sure most of us would try to make contact. I often think of June, the Canadian girl I travelled with for over six months. I'd love to make contact with her but how. I don't even know her surname. "

"Yes, I see your point," Cheryl replied, "But I think it's more than that. Anyway, I've got to go. I'm late already. Joel's got maths tutoring. Call me if anything happens."

Later that afternoon, a chilled chardonnay in hand, I went out to my front verandah, sat down on the cushioned timber bench and looked down over my garden. Rosellas were hopping around in the grevilleas, whilst the lorikeets fed noisily from the birdfeeder. It was paradise. Well that's how I felt sometimes. At other times it seemed more like my prison. I was downhearted. I was approaching fifty. My marriage was over but we were both scared of facing the inevitable. Another two years and Matt would be finished school. Two more years of this. And then what? What would I do?

I could hear Matt in his bedroom playing his guitar. He'd obviously given up on his homework for the moment. He'll be hungry, I thought. I should start to think about this evening's dinner.

I thought about Murat. Maybe I could chat with him one more time before Steve came home. Maybe tomorrow morning I'll go online and see if he pops up. I certainly wasn't looking forward to Christmas but would do my best to get through it for the boys. I'd already made a couple dozen mince pies but needed to do another dozen at least. The Christmas cake was wrapped up and soaking in some brandy in the bottom of the fridge. I had everything pretty much under control. Matt was getting speakers for his Mp3 player and Ben wanted an electric drill for university. Easy, shopping was done. I'd got Steve a couple of t-shirts, but knew he wouldn't get me anything. Maybe he'd get me a book, I mused.

****

"Hello, Zoe. How are you today?" typed Murat.

After I kissed Matt goodbye and waved him off, I pulled out the cable and connected to the internet.

"I'm good, thanks. And you?" I typed back.

"Great," he answered, "I'm very tired but very pleased to be chatting with you. You are my energy. I worked through the night. I'll go home soon and eat something and sleep. What are you doing today?"

"Today I need to mow the lawns and wash the car. I only work three mornings a week these days." I answered. "And, it's Christmas here next week and I'll be super busy with my family, so I won't be able to chat again till after the New Year."

"Ah, okay. I understand," he typed, "I will look forward to the new year. I will be working as usual. But I will think of you," he continued. "Do you ever think back to that night we first met at that little taverna in Nafplio? It was so long ago."

"Yes, of course," I replied.

It seemed like another lifetime ago. Just lately I had been thinking about those days a lot. Those early days when I was young and free, no responsibilities, no one to answer to, just that incredibly sweet feeling of freedom. I think I was really happy in those days. I was living the life I wanted. I was travelling, exploring and meeting lots of new and interesting people. And yes, I had met Murat.

"Do you remember the picnic? And after, the first time I kissed you?" he typed.

1980

Chapter Seven

The springtime sun shimmered on the water and was beckoning us to swim, but the water was still very fresh. Only the guys braved the cool pristine sea, whilst Lynn and I were content to soak up the rays and enjoy the entertainment. The guys had stripped off and were screaming as they ran down the beach and dove into the depths, playing like school boys.

It had been a perfect day. The small and unspoilt little bay was all ours. Surrounded by rocky outcrops and framed perfectly against the bluest sky, we had found a piece of paradise for our picnic.

The walk down from the hostel had passed through many orchards and we had collected a dozen or more oranges that had fallen from the trees and now lay colourfully at their feet. We had a huge loaf of fresh Greek bread, a massive chunk of white cheese, a bag of locally grown cucumbers and of course, a bag of large juicy Kalamata olives. A few bottles of cheap retsina and our picnic was a banquet.

Lynn and I had time to discuss Murat whilst the guys played.

"He is cute," she said, "and he looks fairly fit."

I couldn't have agreed more.

Maybe I was infatuated but Lynn could see the attraction. After all, he was incredibly handsome and he did have an air of mystique. Watching him push his body through the water and then sprint up the beach, I was once again mesmerised. I threw him his towel, which he caught with a smile. That smile was hypnotic.

Prior to flying to London and our meeting, Lynn had just called off her engagement to her high school sweet heart. She knew that they were too young and she wanted to experience life before settling down and starting a family. At this point, her breakup was still raw and the thought of any new romance was very unlikely. But she could see the magnetism I felt towards Murat and she was fine with it. She reassured me that she was just thrilled to be in Greece enjoying the sun, reading her book, and writing her diary. If any romance happened between

Murat and me, it wasn't a problem. I had the green light from my travel buddy.

With his towel wrapped around his waist, he grabbed an orange and took a seat in the sand close to me. This was perfect, I thought. As he peeled the orange, the sweetness of its scent drifted to my nose. My mouth watered in anticipation and caused me to swallow. I felt a chill down my spine. It seemed that all my senses were awakened.

"You like?" he offered me some of his orange and I gladly accepted.

"Water very cold," he stated.

John and Simon were now coming up the beach also, their bodies red from the cold water. They grabbed their towels and with their childish banter and towel slapping, broke the mood and any chance of Murat and I having a special moment together.

The breeze was picking up now and I could feel the goose bumps on my arms. It was then that Murat touched me.

"You are cold?" he asked as he rubbed my arms.

"A little," I replied enjoying his attention and not making any move to get my jumper.

"What a magnificent day it's been," I declared.

"It's not over yet," replied John. "Still a couple hours till sunset, do we still have retsina?"

"Sure," I said, passing him a bottle and a plastic cup.

At this point Murat had moved away and was dressing himself and shaking his hair in the breeze.

"Zoe," he beckoned "You know castle? You come walk?"

I gathered that he was inviting me to walk up to the castle with him.

"Sure," I replied "That will be lovely."

Lynn shot me a wicked smile.

I had seen the castle up on the hill, massive and imposing, looking down on the little sea port. I imagined that it would afford uninterrupted views from the top. I was eager to accompany Murat on this venture and to be able to have some time alone with him, away from the others. Surely John and Simon could feel the energy of our attraction but then again they were guys. It would probably take them a while to pick up on anything. Throughout the Magic Bus ordeal they had been like our big brothers and there wasn't ever the slightest hint of romance, but with Murat it was different.

Leaving the others down on the beach we made our way to the path that would take us to the top of the hill where the castle sat magnificently. The placard at the bottom, told us that there were nine hundred and ninety nine steps to the top.

"There are many steps," I told Murat as I showed him the number. He smiled back at me.

"You want?" he asked.

"Well we can try. Maybe I can't make it. Maybe you must carry me," I joked.

He gently took my hand and off we set, up the massive staircase. We stopped occasionally along the way to save our breath and admire the view at every vantage point. At every turn along the way, we gazed back down upon the steps that we had already conquered. The sea was sparkling and numerous fishing boats dotted the horizon. A small stone fortress sat proudly in the bay. The sun looked huge as it slowly sank and reflected a golden stream of light across the water.

I felt alive and exhilarated. We continued up the steps, determined to make it to the top to witness the sun sink below the horizon. I saw small beads of sweat on Murat's brow. The climb was fairly strenuous and whilst moments before I had been cold, now I too was sweating. The breeze was a welcome relief. We powered on. The sky was beginning to turn a pinkish colour. We had chatted a little along the way, but most of the time we were comfortable in our silence and just the sounds of the sea below us. We didn't have a care in the world, just the thought of completing our mission to reach the top. Our stairway to heaven.

The ancient stone steps showed us the way. Who had climbed these steps before? How old was this castle? It was obvious to us that the location of this castle up on a treacherously rocky crag would have been extremely effective in defending the town from any seafaring enemies as well as providing unbroken views of the areas surrounding Nafplio. We were starting to weary.

At last, the summit was in sight. A few more flights of these ancient stones and we would be there, on top of the world, able to look down at the picturesque town below us and the breath-taking sunset and sea. We were tired but finally triumphant in our quest to conquer the nine hundred and ninety nine steps. We smiled and high fived. We had made it and it felt good.

Gazing out now to the sky and sea, we were silent, just catching our breath and lost in our thoughts and meditation. It was a great victory to have reached the top and our reward was the far reaching views stretched out before us. Together we had shared this journey and created a memory.

I was starting to chill again and Murat put his arm around me and pulled me close. I could feel the warmth of his body through his shirt. My heart was pounding inside my ribcage and I was sure I had a stomach full of butterflies. After gazing aimlessly out to sea, comfortable in the calm, we both turned to each other, caught up in the romance of the moment. Gently, he pulled me closer and looked deeply into my eyes. I was hypnotised. His scent excited me. I could smell the sea on his body and in his hair, the salt still clinging to him. The sound of the sea below was our music. Ever so softly he touched my cheek, all the while looking intensely into my soul. I could hear his breathing now and feel his breath. My gaze drifted from his eyes to his lips, his soft beard and moustache. The world had stopped still for us at this moment.

Slowly and tenderly he moved closer and I felt the warmth of his lips on mine. Our first kiss.

2007

Chapter Eight

"Happy New Year!" I typed.

Christmas had come and gone. Steve and I had managed to refrain from arguing. Still I was thankful to see his car pull out of the driveway and honk his customary goodbye. Ben was home from university for a few more weeks and it warmed my heart to see the boys hanging out together again. As Ben now had his driver's licence they often drove out to the beach or went into town to meet some friends.

At other times they had their friends over to our house so that they could jam out in the garage. We had converted the old garage into a music room and it had a drum kit, a couple of amplifiers, mics, guitars, tambourines, pedals, just about everything they needed to make a lot of loud music. I loved those days. They would be rocking out a new tune and I would be doing some house work or preparing something for them to eat. Teenage boys are always hungry. After a heavy jam session, they would all dive into the pool to cool down, screaming and splashing. Most of the time we would simply throw some sausages on to the barbecue and they would make sausage sandwiches. They were joyful days. The boys were happy. I was happy.

Of course, I was so happy to have both of my boys at home with me. But I felt another sort of happy, a feeling of happiness mixed with anticipation. Some days I felt as if I was floating on air. I just couldn't help myself from smiling. I couldn't stop myself from dancing and singing along to the new Triple JJJ's Hottest One Hundred album, one of the boys' Christmas presents. I began to look forward to my next chat with Murat. I started to let go of my cautiousness and guardedness. I guess at first I had been slightly suspicious as to why he had contacted me. Also the fact that I was hiding our chats from Steve made me feel guilty. Why? It felt like I was having an affair, the thrill of secrecy. But of course, I wasn't. We had only chatted a couple of times. Just two old friends getting in touch again. And anyway, Murat was on the other side of the globe, over ten thousand kilometres away. What could ever come from that?

"Happy New Year to you too," he typed back. "How is everything down under?"

I laughed. I hated that phrase 'the land down under'.

"All good here, still quite hot though," I replied. "What about you?"

"Here we have had snow. Our winter is heavy this year," he replied.

We chatted on for at least an hour or more. We shared what we had been doing over the last couple of weeks. Being a Muslim country, there was no Christmas in Turkey. Life went on as usual. Murat had been working and on his days off he tried to catch up on sleep. He took his sister shopping and just everyday life as normal. He did mention that his wife had now filed for divorce and a court date had been set.

I hadn't yet told him about my situation. He only knew that my husband worked in another city and came home on the odd weekend and that he had been home for Christmas. I don't know why I didn't want to tell him that we were also separated. Perhaps because I thought that, that would present the possibility of rekindling our relationship and I certainly didn't want that.

We were chatting more frequently now. We were delving deeper into each other's pasts. I explained that I had met Steve not long after returning to Australia. We had travelled a bit through Europe by motorbike and even visited Turkey. Our memories of Turkey were precious; children giving us flowers, the shoe shine man down by the docks trying to clean our very dirty biker boots, taking the car ferry from Istanbul to Izmir, all truly awesome memories, colourful and exciting. The food had been incredible and the people so friendly. We had always said that we would return to Turkey one day. We had other travels through Asia and around Australia, but by 1987 we had decided to marry and start a family. Our babies gave us so much joy and they were blissful days, but life had become more routine, more worries and so many more responsibilities.

For Murat, he explained that his life hadn't been as rosy. He had eventually returned to Turkey and as he had expected, he was arrested at the border. He spent some time in prison and was then forced to do his military service. After his initial training in Diyarbakir, he was sent to a town called Hakkari close to the Iraqi border. It was a very dangerous place to be as there were daily skirmishes with the Kurds and winter had been treacherous. Freezing conditions, not much sleep and many soldiers had lost their lives. In due course, he returned wearily to his family home near Rize on the Black Sea.

It had then become his mother's task to find him a wife and that's how he ended up marrying Asli, the daughter of a friend of his mother's cousin. They hadn't even held hands before the wedding. They were complete strangers but his mother had liked her and so it was, they married and had a big fat traditional Turkish wedding. The party had gone on through the night with much feasting, fireworks, music and dancing. The entire village was invited and everyone cheered the happy couple.

His mother had told him, that in time, they would grow to love each other and she looked forward to them giving her many grandchildren. Her wish had come true and not long after their wedding, Asli became pregnant with their first son, and then a couple of years later their second son arrived.

Murat had worked in his father's market and he had also helped harvest the hazel nuts from their family plot. Life on the Black Sea had been easy enough but he couldn't see a future. He wanted more. His time spent in Greece had shown him a different life, different from the slow village existence he was at that time, living. He had spent a couple of seasons working on the cargo boats and travelled up and down the African coastline visiting many exotic places. Now here he was living the village life, still under the watchful eye of his parents. He didn't want that anymore. Did he want his boys to grow up as villagers without proper education or any career goals? Was harvesting hazelnuts their future?

He had then begun looking at his employment options. He had accrued plenty of experience working on the fishing boats and cargo boats. It wasn't long until he found his current job, monitoring the passage of all water crafts along the Bosphorus, which connected the Black Sea to the Sea of Marmara, and Asia to Europe.

It paid well but meant leaving the Black Sea and Asli did not want to leave her family. Basically that's when the cracks started to appear in their marriage, as she became depressed and distant. He had bought her a lovely home in a small town on the Dardanelles, commuting distant to Istanbul. The kids had gone to an excellent school and were content and doing well but she just wasn't happy. She became lazy and spent her days watching Turkish soap operas and dating programs on the massive television that she had wanted. She began to want more and more, spending his hard earned savings on designer clothes and shoes. She began to neglect her home duties and often when he returned home from a long night shift, there was no meal prepared for him. He wanted to sleep but the television was always blaring and of course, the arguments started.

Listening to Murat's story, I felt sad for the hardships he had suffered. A few years earlier, his mother had passed away from cancer and his sister had just recently overcome breast cancer and was for now, in the clear. As we chatted over the coming months, new pieces of the puzzle fell into place; we had almost twenty seven years of our lives to catch up on.

"So, do you ever think back to Athens? Our last time together? That special time we shared? " he asked one day.

Those memories were bringing back sensations that I hadn't felt for a very long time. His reminiscences were stirring up long buried feelings and emotions. How could I ever forget those days?

"Well I hadn't thought about them for quite a while," I admitted, "but since you are bringing them up, I guess I will think more about them now."

"Darling, is it okay if I call you darling?" he asked.

"Oh I don't know, why?" I replied. I was feeling uneasy. He had crossed the line now. What did calling me 'darling' mean? It meant that instead of simply chatting to an old friend, we would be chatting as romantic partners, lovers.

"Can you give me your telephone number, I need to hear your voice," he asked.

I was feeling uncomfortable and even slightly threatened. It would be exciting to hear his voice too but would it mean that I am succumbing to his charms and starting an affair. It was feeling like an affair now. Still I rationalised; he is over ten thousand kilometres away, he can't touch me through the computer or phone. We are just talking. I am separated after all. I felt the warmth rise from my neck to my cheeks. What was I doing? Was this right? My brain was saying it wasn't right, but my heart was saying otherwise.

"Ok", I said.

1980

Chapter Nine

We had never intended on staying in Nafplio for so long, but Lynn was content to chill and I was ecstatic to spend my days and nights with Murat. John and Simon had moved on to the next archaeological site on their Greek odyssey and we had promised to try and catch up with them later back in the United Kingdom.

My time spent with Murat was like a dream; lazy days picnicking down on the beach, walking through the local orchards, and enjoying all the local cuisine at our favourite beach taverna. But all good things have to come to an end and Lynn was expressing her wishes to continue our travels and besides that, Murat seriously needed to find work.

Our goodbye was painful and I cried so much, but I had committed to travelling with Lynn and she had been patient enough. We boarded the bus and Murat sadly waved us goodbye. I felt like I was abandoning him. I had given him my details, my mother's address in Australia and the Colonial Club Hotel address in London.

"Write to me," I said.

We would be back in London in a few weeks as Lynn was booked on an around Europe bus tour, twelve countries in a massive thirty five days, camping most of the way. It was organised by the Colonial Club and was very well priced. Maybe I could do it too.

"Come on, we could share a tent. I don't want to share with a stranger. Think of all the fun we'd have," Lynn pleaded.

It was true that we did get on really well and I agreed that it could be loads of fun. We had shown Murat the itinerary and he knew the days that we would arrive in Athens. He also planned on going to Athens as there was more chance of finding a job on a fishing boat there. So our tentative plans were made.

"I'll see you again in Athens," I said as I kissed him farewell. If it was meant to be, we would hook up again in Athens. It gave us both hope and something to look forward to.

Tears streaming down my cheeks, I waved through the window and blew kisses, as our bus pulled onto the road. I watched as Murat stood there alone, waving, until he was out of view.

"Cheer up," said Lynn "You two will be back together before you know it."

"I hope so," I mumbled back deep in thought.

****

So far the organised bus tour through Europe had been a blast; a lot of partying and a lot of alcohol went down. There were about thirty people on the tour all aged between eighteen and thirty, but most were around the early twenties like us. They came from a mix of countries but most were Australians, a couple of Canadians and a few Americans. The coach was large and very comfortable, absolutely no comparison to our Magic Bus experience. In fact, on this bus, it was so comfortable that we often found ourselves dozing off and catching up on the sleep we missed from the previous night's parties and shenanigans. Before we knew it we were in a new city and a new camp site.

All the camping gear was stored in the back of the bus and it was up to each couple to erect their tent and get organised before dinner. We were all on a roster system for either cooking, serving or washing up. Sheila and Jack, the tour guide and organiser, usually bought all the food at the local markets and together with those rostered on for cooking, prepared the most scrumptious meals. Mick, the driver was also a good sport and if he wasn't flirting with the girls, he was helping with the cooking too. The entire tour was a well organised and very enjoyable experience despite its long duration.

Lynn and I had become quite fond of our tent. We'd bought extra warm sleeping bags when we were back in London. Some nights were freezing, especially running from a steaming hot shower through the cold night air and into our cold tents but luckily after a few moments we were as snug as little bugs in a rug. As we travelled through northern Europe it had been cold and damp but as we started to head south, the sun came out again and the temperatures began to rise.

Even Serbia and Macedonia didn't seem as scary as they had whilst travelling through on the Magic Bus; those disgusting roadhouse restaurants and the aggressive police at the border crossings. This time around, the border crossings were a breeze as Sheila and Jack took care of everything. I was counting the days till we would arrive in Athens. I had received one letter from Murat back in London and he had said that he was now living in Athens, sharing a flat with a guy he had met on the boats. He said he would be waiting for me at the Acropolis, but that just seemed too random. But then how else would we find each other? It was our best bet. After all, every tour bus would be heading to Athens's greatest tourist attraction.

As we were travelling through northern Greece, I was becoming anxious.

"What if I miss him? What if I never see him again?" I cried to Lynn.

"You won't miss him. He'll be there. Don't worry," she reassured me.

"And what should I do when I do meet him? We are in Athens for three days. Do you think I can skip off and stay with him? Will they let me?" I asked for Lynn's opinion.

"It could be an insurance problem if you left, but if you explained that you would be safe with your boyfriend, maybe they would allow it," she replied. "I think you have to tell Sheila and Jack. It wouldn't be fair to just disappear and scare them."

"Yeah," I agreed.

Sure as sure, as we finally arrived in Athens, the first attraction our bus took us to was the majestic Acropolis. I eagerly scampered off the bus, all the time looking around, searching the crowds. We were not the only tour bus there and massive hordes of tourists were clambering over the ancient stones of the Acropolis. We had obviously come at peak time for tour buses and tourists in general. It hadn't been this crazy when we were last here.

Lynn and I were with a group of our friends from the tour. We too joined the throng of tourists making their way to the top. Even though I had been here just a few months earlier, I was still in awe of this ancient citadel. As I looked around it seemed ludicrous to me that Murat and I could have ever thought that we would find each other here. I felt deflated.

"Don't give up just yet. We have only just arrived," remarked Lynn. "Give him a chance. He'll find us."

I wished I could be as optimistic as her but it didn't look good. It was peak time and peak crowds.

We wandered around together, everyone laughing and happy to be in Athens. A couple of the guys were being silly as usual but I couldn't laugh. I tried to join in the merriment but instead I felt irritated by all the noise and jollity. My thoughts were elsewhere. How could I find him, I was thinking? How could we have possibly thought that we could meet here?

Lynn heard it first. Then I heard it. Was it my name?

"Zoe, Zoe," he called.

We turned and carefully examined the crowd; all the tourists looked the same, cameras around their necks, sun hats on, daypacks and water bottles.

"Zoe," he called again. Again we scanned the crowd.

Then we saw him. He was running up through the pack.

"Murat. My God, it's you. You found me," I screamed as I ran towards him. He threw his arms around me and practically lifted me off the ground. It seemed like our embrace lasted for ever. His hairline and brow were running with sweat, but his eyes were as sparkling as I remembered. He looked tanned and more nourished than the last time I had seen him. He had regular work and could afford to eat well now. His hair was longer and blonder with the sun. We kissed.

"You look great," I said.

"You too," he replied. "Miss you much. Long time."

"Yes," I agreed, "I was scared that you wouldn't find me. But you did. We are together again. Unbelieveable."

After our initial embrace, we soon realised that we had a small audience. Lynn and the rest of our friends from the tour were looking on and waiting for me to introduce them.

"Hey everyone, this is Murat," I explained as Lynn gave him a welcoming hug and the others moved in to shake his hand. "Hopefully I'll be spending the next few days with him."

We said our goodbyes and they all resumed their climb to the Parthenon. "Bye Lynn." I said as I gave her a big hug. "See you in three days."

"Have fun. Be good. Enjoy your selves," she replied warmly. We could feel her happiness for us.

We stood alone now, holding hands and staring intensely into each other's eyes, excited at the prospect of three whole days together.

"What will we do now?" I finally asked.

"We go my home, we make food and wine. We celebrate," he said.

I found Sheila and Jack and introduced them to Murat. I explained the situation and they were fine with it as long as I was back the morning of their departure. They didn't want to have to wait for me. I assured them I would be there on time.

"See you in three days," I said excitedly. I couldn't hide my happiness.

"Enjoy your time but remember if you're not here, we leave without you," they said with warm smiles.

And so, for the next three days and nights Murat and I were together again. His flatmate was covering his shifts so that we could have the entire time together, time to relax and catch up on each other's lives.

It was a magical time. Murat showed me around the ancient port area known as the Piraeus. This was where he lived and worked now. This was where all the fishing boats left from as well as all the ferry boats that visited the Greek islands. His flat was small and old but he was proud to show me his home and I was over the moon to be there with him. For the next three days we cooked together, relaxed together, spent the whole day in bed together and imagined what our lives would be like if we lived together. Murat wanted that; to live together, to be together always. He didn't want to lose me again. He loved me and wanted to get married.

I loved him too, but I wasn't ready for such a commitment.

"Murat, I love you too but I'm not ready for marriage," I explained. "I still want to travel and see as much of the world as possible. And anyway, how long can you stay away from your family? You will need to go home one day."

"We can Greece stay. Maybe go your country," he replied.

"Let's take it slow and see what happens," is all I could say. I wasn't ready for marriage. I didn't even think I ever wanted to marry. I was enjoying my freedom too much.

"Murat, let's enjoy this time, the time we have right now," I said as I put my head upon his chest.

2007

Chapter Ten

I was sitting on the front verandah with my morning coffee. It was just after half past seven and Matt had just left to take the school bus. I was expecting Murat's phone call. He had said he would call at this time but I didn't know which phone he'd call; the land line or my mobile, so I had both resting on the table, waiting. I was fiddling with a loose thread on my dressing gown and just gazing down across the garden.

Even though I was expecting his call, I jumped when the phone rang, nearly spilling my coffee. Hesitating just a moment, I picked up the land line phone and answered, "Hello."

"Zoe?" he asked. "Is that you?"

"Yes, Murat, it's me." I said with a hint of eagerness.

"My God," he said "Your voice is good to hear. It is as I remember. You sound the same."

I could detect a slight tremble in his voice but I had to admit, it was thrilling for me also to be talking to him after all these years.

"You sound pretty good too," I remarked.

I could feel the emotion in his voice. I was trying to recall the last time that we had spoken. It was so long ago. Yes, he had called me one night in London. He was upset and had wanted me to come back to Greece, but I was working then and had other travel plans ahead. Gosh, I was a bitch, I thought. How I must have hurt him.

Hearing his voice again now after twenty seven years was moving for me also and a range of memories and thoughts flooded my brain. What if I had gone back to him?

For months now we had chatted online, but this phone call took everything to a different level. This was real. This was happening. He was at work and it was a quiet night on the Bosphorus and here in Australia, I was about to start my day. The call was clear and crisp. It sounded like he was just down the road not over ten thousand kilometres away.

We were fast approaching winter in Australia but the morning sun on my verandah was soothing and warm. In

Turkey they were enjoying springtime but the nights were still cool, he said. He loved springtime the best as did I.

At first, we seemed to be lost for words. Our questions were about the weather and work. On my verandah, I watched as my favourite pair of lorikeets sat on the bird feeder cracking open the sun flower seeds and making little contented sounds. I tried to describe my surroundings to Murat. The vista from my verandah was a picture of colour and nature. Then a massive white cockatoo flew onto the garage roof and squawked at the top of his voice. They loved to attack the cedar finial on the front of the garage.

"My God, what was that?" asked Murat.

I just laughed. "That was a sulphur crested cockatoo. He is a large white bird with a yellow comb on his head and he loves to eat away at the cedar on my house," I replied. "He's a bit of a pest but beautiful too and we feel lucky to have so much wild life where we live."

"Tell me more about where you live," he asked.

"Well, we live in a medium size house that is about twenty years old now. It is a greyish blue weatherboard cottage with dark blue and mauve trim. It has a large verandah all the way around and we are surrounded by five acres of beautiful native trees and gardens," I explained. "It's very serene and my verandah is my favourite place. It's my place of peace."

"That sounds perfect," he sighed. "My family home is a large apartment on the fourth floor. It is modern and is what she wanted. It has two large balconies but they just look into more apartment blocks. It's very comfortable but not as peaceful as I'd like. I always dreamed of a house with a garden. But anyway, now I live with my sister as you know. It is small and old," he replied. "You know, my sister Nihal is divorced and has not got much money. Even after the cancer, she works very hard as a cleaner but they don't pay her well. I help her, of course."

My knowledge of Turkey's social system was not that great but I couldn't imagine that women had it easy there, let alone a divorced woman. It was still a very patriarchal society and women were at the mercy of their male counterparts. Sadly, divorced women were viewed almost as rejects. It must have been very hard for Nihal, I pondered.

Talking with Murat after all these years seemed like a dream. It wasn't long till we both relaxed and it seemed like just yesterday that we had been together. Talking was certainly easier than typing and we were able to share more interesting facts about our countries, more stories about our past. He told me more details about his marriage and his spoilt children, who didn't seem to miss him.

"They just miss my money," he said. "They want their designer sneakers and designer jeans." He was angry and hurt.

Our morning chats soon became a regular occurrence and I looked forward to his calls. I would make my coffee and sit out in the sun waiting for the phone to ring. For me it was a wonderful way to start my day. I knew I was smiling more, laughing more and I wondered if anyone had noticed. Cheryl had.

"You just seem much happier these days, like the huge black cloud above your head has lifted," she observed. And she was right. I did feel like I was walking on sunshine now. I was skipping on sunshine.

But I still questioned whether or not this was an affair? As our conversations became warmer and sometimes cheeky, I began to feel that we had crossed into the realms of an affair. It felt thrilling to be talking this way and to have someone care about my day. Perhaps it was the secrecy of it all, or the feeling that we were crossing into forbidden territory, but I felt alive; alive with excitement. It seemed like my mind and my body were awaking from a long sleep. I felt like a teenager again.

It wasn't long before I finally opened up and told Murat the truth about my marriage; that I was also separated from my husband. It felt like a huge weight had lifted off my shoulders. I tried to explain that nothing had

72

really happened. We didn't have money problems anymore, no one had had an affair but we had just drifted apart. We hadn't slept together for a few years now and we weren't happy living together. We hadn't discussed divorce but it was inevitable. Steve just loved his work and he'd rather be in the office than with me. I had tried many times to reignite some passion. I had suggested weekends away, or to go out for dinner just the two of us, but he was never keen on the idea. There was always something more pressing to do at the office. Anyway, I had given up now and could no longer envisage a future with Steve.

Since we had started talking on phone, we had definitely become closer. We managed to find the opportunity a few times a week to talk. Whilst I sat in the car every Wednesday evening, waiting for Matt to have his maths tutoring session, Murat almost always found the time to call me. I could buzz his phone at any time and within minutes he would call me back.

There were a few occasions when he was not able to get to the phone. One week he was working on a ship out in the Aegean and had little time alone. Another time he had to make a quick trip home to Rize to see his father who was not well. It was on these occasions, we could only text each other. Our texts were becoming more and more loving. He always sent me a 'good night, sweet dreams' text. He always signed off with love and kisses. These texts became precious to me but I also felt like I was really cheating now, having a secret love affair. I changed his name in my phone contacts from Murat to Mary. The likelihood of Steve ever checking my phone was very slim, but still I did it.

"Cheryl, I'm having an affair," I confessed. "And it's your fault. You made me contact him."

"Zoe, it isn't an affair if you are separated from your husband," she laughed.

"It is. I'm not divorced. I'm pretty sure it's an affair," I replied.

"Is there any funny business going on?" she asked. "You know what I mean," she was smiling now. "Any dirty talk?"

I felt embarrassed.

"Really, if anyone had told me that I would be having an affair, I would never have believed it. I'm the least likely person to have an affair. You know that. What's happened to me?" I asked looking seriously at Cheryl.

"Zoe, don't beat yourself up over this. You're human. Everybody wants love and attention and you've found it with Murat. If Steve was different you wouldn't be pursuing this, would you?"

She was right. If I was happily married, of course, I'd never be entertaining another man. And if it didn't feel like romance, I wouldn't be keeping it a secret. It was my big secret and I had to keep everything to myself, but at the same time I wanted to tell everyone. Anyway, I consoled myself, nothing could ever come of this. He's in Turkey and I'm in Australia. We are worlds apart. For the moment it was simply a diversion from my routine life, something to make me smile and give me these precious moments of happiness.

I remembered the woman up in the corner house. I'd forgot her name now but I'd met her through our school community and that was really the only time I saw her or got to say a few words to her. Then she just vanished. No one saw her again. The rumour was that she had been having an online relationship with a guy in the United States and had suddenly just upped and gone to him, leaving behind her husband and son, confused and distraught.

The school crowd could be so bitchy and judgmental. They didn't know all the details, but for a small country town this was big juicy gossip. This gave the canteen ladies amusement for weeks. God, would that be me? Never, I'd never leave my kids. I won't be giving them any gossip material, that's for sure.

Chapter Eleven

"It's my birthday at the end of this month, the big one," I said.

"The big one? You mean forty?" Murat joked.

"I wish," I replied with a giggle. "You know I mean fifty."

Yes, my fiftieth birthday was coming up and it was quite scary to be truthful. My birthdays had always passed without much fuss. I wasn't one for parties and attention. Normally it was just another day. Sometimes I'd bake myself a birthday cake for the kid's sake. For Steve's birthday I'd always bake his favourite Black Forest cherry cake and arrange something special. One time we went to Byron Bay. Another time we went camping. My birthdays didn't attract the same celebrations until the boys got older and then they spoilt me. I remember Ben and Matt taking me to see a Harry Potter movie last year.

But this was my fiftieth birthday. I had reached the top of the mountain and now there was only one way to go. Luckily I was still fit and healthy. I'd lost a few friends over the last couple of years to cancer. You really don't know what's around the corner. So I decided I wanted to do something special for this birthday, something memorable, something grand.

I had a friend in London. Her name was Maria and we had worked together waiting tables at the Merchant Navy Hotel in the early eighties. She was from Columbia and had come to London to learn English and she never left, becoming a fully-fledged British subject now. She proudly owned her own home in North West London and on many occasions she had invited me to come and stay with her. Maybe that could be something to think about.

The truth is I hadn't travelled anywhere solo since the eighties. I was a bit scared of going alone now. Funny how we lose that adventurous spirit with age. I did try to rationalise that really nothing could go wrong as long as I kept my passport and credit card safe.

As a family we had done quite a few adventurous holidays to Asia, Europe and around Australia. Travelling as a family was a rewarding experience, showing our children the world, teaching them things that they could never learn in the classroom. I had always been in charge of the travel bookings, flights and accommodations. I always carried all four passports and all the other necessary documents. I made most of the decisions when it came to our route and where we'd stay. Steve drove the hire car and carried the luggage. It always went quite smoothly and we had never experienced any major hiccups. So if I could organise a party of four, then logically, travelling alone should be much easier. Still, I was slightly anxious and unsure. I had to push myself and step outside of my comfort zone. Who knew what would be out there?

Further correspondence with Maria, and I decided that I would do it. I would fly to London for ten days and then on to Berlin for 5 days more and fly home. My mother was born in Berlin and I had always felt a strong connection to that city. I had last been there in 1985 before the Wall had come down. I was eager to see Berlin now, the modern unified Berlin.

So before I booked anything, I had to run the idea past Steve. I explained that I would go at the beginning of low season and I would be very grateful if he could take two weeks off work to come and look after Matt. It would be an excellent opportunity for him to have one to one time with his son, and he could maybe do some home maintenance jobs, not that anything really needed doing. He seemed okay with the idea and I booked my flights.

Maria would meet me at Heathrow airport and we both looked forward to this reunion. I needed to book a hotel or a guest house in Berlin and then my plans were set.

"And how will you celebrate your fiftieth birthday?" he asked.

"Well, I'm thinking to go and visit a friend of mine in London," I replied. "I haven't travelled alone for so long, I'm a bit scared," I confessed.

"Nothing to be scared about," he said. "You are a strong woman."

Yes, I thought, I am a strong woman and of course I can do it. What's there to be scared about?

"How long do you plan to be away," he asked.

"I will have ten days in London and five days in Berlin. Not too long. Steve has to take leave from work and come and look after Matt," I replied.

"Hmm, very nice," Murat sighed. "It will be good for you."

"What did you do for your fiftieth?" I asked.

"You know here in Turkey, we don't care so much about birthdays. Mine was a couple of years before and I think I just went to work as usual," he explained.

We continued talking about my travel plans and now that it was really going to happen, I was getting excited. Murat was excited for me also. I now felt I could tell him anything and everything. He was a patient listener and I realised how much I had missed someone to talk to, someone to confide in and someone who cared.

Over our next few morning calls, I eagerly explained my travel plans; what I planned to do in London and how I planned to spend my days in Berlin. I described the quaint little 'Gasthaus' that I had booked for my stay in Berlin and how I was looking forward to visiting the many new museums that had opened since the fall of the Wall. I had planned to find the house where my mother had grown up in and take some photos for her. Berlin had so much for me to see and do, and I loved German food, heavy and rich but so delicious.

In London, I looked forward to my days with Maria, visiting the British museum and definitely enjoying a traditional British pub lunch. I had lived in London for a few years so I wasn't that interested in seeing all the tourist sights again, but probably a ride on the new London Eye would be novel. It was exciting times and I felt lifted. I was counting down the weeks till my departure.

"Why don't you make a stopover in Istanbul?" he asked.

Chapter Twelve

Istanbul, a stopover in Istanbul? Not possible. No way. My flights were booked, everything was arranged. Why would he suggest that? I was confused.

"Why would he suggest that?" I asked Cheryl. "Why would he come up with such a stupid idea? He's spoilt everything now."

"Zoe, listen to yourself. You are panicking about nothing," she replied. "Why wouldn't he suggest it? It makes sense. You are over in his hemisphere and it's an opportunity for both of you to meet up. I think it makes perfect sense and you should do it," she continued.

"I should do it? Meet up with a previous boyfriend and lover? Even though I'm still technically married?" I hammered Cheryl with my questions.

"Yes," she replied firmly. "You should do it."

"Zoe, life is so short and if we don't take chances like this, we might miss some mind blowing opportunities. Maybe this is meant to be. Maybe this is fate. You deserve this after so many unhappy years. Murat makes you smile and so I say 'Do it'," she continued.

I sighed. This was heavy for me. "What if he's a serial killer now?" I asked.

"You are just being silly. I understand that you are scared but try and think logically. It would be so good for you. Next time you talk, tell him that you are considering his offer and ask him just what did he have in mind?" she suggested.

The more I mulled over the idea, the more I could see Cheryl's reasoning. I guess it did make sense. A short stopover in Istanbul would be reasonable. I'd get a hotel and we could meet for dinner and keep everything above board. A couple of days in Istanbul would mean I could visit the Grand Bazaar and buy the kids some presents. Okay yes, I had convinced myself now. I would speak with him first and then see if my agent could change my flights.

****

"Hi, Murat, how are you this morning?"

His call was always punctual. I was sitting in my lounge room looking out through the massive glass panes at the driving rain that was hitting my verandah. The pair of love bird lorikeets was huddled together on a rafter, trying to escape the cold downpour. I had moved the feeder to a dry place but they hadn't yet noticed its new location. It was going to be a wet few days.

"I am well, my darling," he replied. "How about you?"

"I am well too. I have been thinking about your suggestion," I explained.

"Yes, me too," he said. "If you come I will take holidays and we will drive to Cappadocia. Have you ever been there? Do you know it?"

Again, I was taken aback. First it was a couple of days in Istanbul and now it was a holiday to Cappadocia.

"Cappadocia," I exclaimed. "Yes, I have heard of it. I have seen pictures and it looks out of this world. But Murat, I don't think I can take a holiday with you."

"But why not?" he questioned.

"Because.......because it's not right. Because I am still a married woman and a mother, and I can't be away so long."

"You are scared? Zoe, your marriage is as good as over, like mine. You can cut short your days in London and have five or six days with me," he pleaded. "You know I have always loved you and have thought about you for ever. It is my greatest wish to see you again and take you to Cappadocia. It will be an adventure, our adventure. Come on, Zoe, just think about it."

Again, I felt torn. A part of me wanted this so bad, but another part of me told me it was wrong. The sensible part of my brain told me that I would be cheating and this wasn't my character. The more emotional side of my brain thought how exhilarating and romantic this would be; driving through Anatolia with my long lost lover to the mysterious and spectacular landscapes of Cappadocia.

My brain was exploding with indecision. Normally a logical decisive person, able to make snap judgements, I was now faced with a decision that I couldn't take lightly. This decision could have long reaching consequences.

In my heart of hearts I desperately wanted this. I needed this. Murat made me feel alive and I knew that a few days together would be therapeutic and liberating. For years now there had been no intimacy in my marriage and the thought of being touched and loved by a man again sent shivers down my spine.

"Let me think about it," I said as our phone session came to an end.

Chapter Thirteen

"Okay," I said with gusto. I hadn't taken this decision lightly and I had agonised for days, but eventually I had come to terms with the idea and just decided to go with it.

"Okay? Are you telling me that you will come to Turkey? That you will visit me?" replied Murat, his voice bouncing down the phone line. "Darling, this will be amazing."

"Yes, Murat, I'm telling you that I will come to Turkey and we can go to Cappadocia," I replied. I could feel my heart racing and my skin tingling. Now that I had made the decision, I felt an enormous release of pressure and I couldn't believe just how excited I felt.

I would need to make some changes to my booking. I'd need to shorten my stay with Maria and shorten my stop in Berlin. The hardest part would be telling Steve that I had decided to add a few days in Turkey to my itinerary and that I might consider Cappadocia as my fiftieth birthday present. After all, he knew how much I had always wanted to go there.

Back in 1985, when we had been travelling through Turkey by motorbike, I had seen posters of Cappadocia at the camp sites and hostels. I had desperately wanted to go there then but Steve had said that it was too far away and he was keen to stay on the coast.

Also, he was keen to stay travelling with this other biker couple that we had met at the camp site in Yeşilyurt. It had been our very first evening in Istanbul and when we pulled into the campsite and began to set up our tent, this young German couple arrived shortly after on a big BMW bike, similar to ours. We had started chatting and after a fun evening together at a nearby restaurant, we had all decided to travel together. They planned to take the car ferry to Izmir and then travel down as far as Antalya. It sounded like a reasonable itinerary and it ended with taking the car ferry from the very picturesque port town of Marmaris to the Greek island of Rhodes. Consequently I didn't get to see Cappadocia. So, I reasoned, the idea that I was now going to have a few days in Cappadocia did seem feasible.

Steve was fine with my change of plans and a few extra days away. He could never have imagined what my plans really were. My conscience wasn't clear and I felt heavy with guilt but as Cheryl had said, "he doesn't make any effort to reconcile your marriage woes and he just takes you for granted."

She was right. Sometimes, I swear he didn't even see me anymore. I could be walking around naked and he wouldn't notice. It would never ever dawn on him that I was having an affair and I was quite sure now that I was having an affair.

Of course, I could tell him the truth but what would that accomplish. I wanted to wait till Matt had finished high school. I didn't want to disturb his studies with the trauma of his parent's divorce. I just needed to keep it all under wraps for another year. In the meantime, I deserved this holiday and I deserved the love and attention of Murat.

****

He called me the night before my flight to Istanbul. I'd just got in from dinner at a little German restaurant around the corner. I'd indulged in some typical German fare; rouladen, dumplings and a little red cabbage, followed by apple strudel and fresh cream. I'd even ordered a glass of Moselle to compliment my meal and ease my growing anxiety.

I had enjoyed my time in both London and Berlin, but they were just the appetisers in this feast of adventure and exploration that lay before me. Of course, it was brilliant seeing Maria again and catching up on news but I actually felt like I had been wishing those days away. I tried to relax and enjoy the moment but the whole time my mind was on Istanbul and Murat. It was the prize at the end of the road. That's what it had all come down to now.

I had given him my Berlin hotel's name and number and they had put the call through to my room. I jumped when the phone on the bed side table shrilled. We hadn't spoken for so long now. During my time in London and here in Berlin we had only used text messages. It was difficult for me to predict my movements as in London I was with Maria most of the time and in Berlin I was always busy and had so much to see. To hear his voice again brought goose bumps to my skin and my heart was racing as I anticipated our reunion tomorrow.

"Darling, I've missed you," he said. "Tomorrow we shall celebrate. We will be together again. Am I dreaming?"

"No, you're not dreaming," I replied warmly. "This is happening. I can't believe it myself."

We chatted a little longer about my time in Berlin and about his plans to leave the office and meet me at the airport. Then he had the next six days off work so that we could spend this precious time together.

"Okay, sleep well my darling. Tomorrow I will meet you and we will begin our journey together. Be calm and relax. Everything will be fine, you'll see," he reassured me. "I kiss you". His words were warm and soothing. I could sense the joy in his voice. Tomorrow we would be reunited after twenty seven years.

Chapter Fourteen

As my Turkish Airline's plane landed at Istanbul's Atatürk Airport, I could feel the knots in my stomach tighten just that bit more. I had enjoyed a wine during the flight from Berlin, but it did little to calm my nerves. A combination of anxiety and anticipation churned my stomach and caused me to break out into a sweat. It was hot on the plane. We were taxiing towards the terminal and it seemed to take for ever.

Finally, the plane came to a complete halt and strangely, this was followed by cheers and claps from the passengers. I hadn't experienced that before. Eventually the seat belt sign turned off and there was a surge of activity as people jumped to remove their belongings from the overhead lockers. I grappled for mine and found my place in the aisle, waiting for some movement, waiting for the line to inch forward so that we could disembark, eager to begin this adventure. I turned on my mobile phone and waited as the messages loaded; messages from my sons, a message from Cheryl and of course, a message from Murat.

'Welcome to Turkey.'

****

Last night had been difficult. I couldn't sleep. After Murat's call I tried to relax. He had sounded so sweet and overjoyed. He sounded like a child with a surprise present to open. What if he was disappointed? He had organised our holiday and I had nothing to worry about, he said. But I did worry. I worried about whether we would get on together. I worried about cheating on my husband. I worried about my looks. What if he didn't find me attractive anymore? What if I didn't find him attractive anymore?

We had, of course, sent each other photos of ourselves. I had chosen the best I had, as I'm sure he did. Photos can be deceiving. I was fifty years old now and he was almost fifty three. My body had seen a lot of changes since the twenty two year old Zoe that he had known. I had put on a few kilos, a bit of cellulite here and there and my breasts had taken a general shift south. I looked in the mirror, scrutinising myself. There were a few wrinkles around the eyes. I just had to accept that the lines on my face were the product of my life from my happy times to the gloomy ones.

And what if I didn't find him attractive? We would be together for nearly a week. What about sleeping together? I'm sure that was on the agenda. Of course, it was. God, I couldn't imagine it. I hadn't been with any man except Steve for the past twenty three years. It would definitely be strange. Even if we had been lovers before, maybe we felt different this time around.

I tried to sleep as I needed to look at least fresh when I saw him again for the first time. I consoled myself with the thought that if it didn't work out well, I could just catch the next plane home. I could just tell Steve that I was homesick.

****

As I made my way to the exit doors, I could feel my heart racing and my palms sweating. The heat was rising up to my face and I felt flushed. I thought to myself, this was a stupid idea, coming to Turkey to meet a man I hardly know.

As I walked through the exit doors, I was greeted by a throbbing and colourful crowd of dark haired olive skinned men and covered women eagerly waiting to welcome home their family members. The crowd was maybe six people deep. How would I find Murat in this mob? I knew I had to get clear of the crowd and find some space alone. I saw a Gloria Jean's coffee shop to my right and made my way there. It was early evening and the airport was hectic and loud. People were calling out to their loved ones, emotional family reunions, grandmas, children, crying babies all adding to the chaos. I pushed my way through, towards the coffee shop, pulling my suitcase along behind me. I was approached many times by men asking if I needed their shuttle service to my hotel.

"Taksim? Sultanahmet? Madam, where your hotel?"

"I'm waiting for a friend," I replied. "I don't need a shuttle, thank you."

The hustle and bustle was stressful and annoying. I found a comfortable easy chair and took refuge there, relieved to be out of the crowds. It was too late in the day for me to have a coffee, I thought. I needed water and momentarily left my suitcase alone to purchase a bottle. I only had euros but luckily they accepted my money.

Another message from Murat had just arrived, 'I'm parking now. Much traffic. Be there soon.'

I was grateful for these moments to clear my head and centre myself. Okay, I am what I am, I told myself. If he doesn't find me attractive there is nothing I can do about it. My head was full of silly thoughts and I wished I was at home sitting on my verandah with a chardonnay in hand.

Normally I loved airports; watching the other travellers, wondering where they were going to or where they had come from. Airports made me feel alive; apart of the big world, moving from country to country. However, tonight I felt tired and anxious. What had I done, I asked myself. What the hell was I thinking? I needed to calm down. I tried deep breathing and focusing on my breath. Relax, I told myself. It's too late to back out now, so just go with the flow. I could always depend on my intuition. If it didn't feel right, I would get a hotel for the night and fly home tomorrow. Yes, easy solution. Relax, you've got this, I convinced myself.

I saw him first.

My God, I could recognise him that easily? All these years and yet I could still pick him out of the crowd? Yes, it was him. I was sure.

"Murat," I called as I got up and began to approach him. "Murat."

He turned and saw me.

His steps quickened, as he walked towards me. His smile was the first thing I noticed, the same charismatic smile that I had been attracted to all those years before, the same beautiful smile that had always made my heart melt. I felt giddy. All the noise and chaos of the arrival's terminal faded away and it was just us.

"Zoe, my Zoe," he called as he approached me with open arms. I felt the safety and comfort of his embrace. Strong and powerful, he held me tight for some moments. As he slowly withdrew his grip, he looked deep into my eyes and kissed me. His eyes were ringed with moisture. I could feel his love and all my anxiety and doubts just washed away. I knew in that instant that this was meant to be.

"Zoe, I'm so happy that you came. You look as beautiful as I remember," he said, his voice slightly quivering. He held my hands and we looked long at each other. He laughed. "This is my dream come true. I can't believe that you are really here."

"So, how was your flight?" he asked as we once more became aware of our surroundings. "Would you like something to drink now or should we get out of here?"

He explained how he had finished up work that afternoon, gone back to his sister's home to shower and then drove out to the airport but the traffic had been horrendous.

"It's quite normal in Istanbul, but we can never predict just how long our journey will take," he apologised. "But I have you now," he added with a beaming smile as he gathered up my luggage.

We made small chat as he led me to his car.

"Tonight we will stay in a classic Ottoman hotel in Istanbul. I'm sure you will love it. And tomorrow we will begin our journey to Cappadocia. Is that okay with you?" he asked.

"Sure, that sounds perfect," I said. "At the moment I am desperately looking forward to a nice warm shower."

"You shall have soon," he replied. "Are you hungry? We can go out for dinner or order up room service, whatever you want. Words cannot describe how I feel to have you here, my darling."

Whilst he was driving I had the opportunity to study him closely. His hair was a lot darker now, peppered with grey. It was still longish but stylish. He was clean shaved and had deep set wrinkles around his eyes and forehead. I would get him to grow back the beard, I thought.

He was dressed in well-fitting jeans and a black polo t-shirt. He still looked fit and he was still very attractive to me. I just hoped that he felt the same, but from his warm welcome, I think he did.

"I'm pretty tired. I think room service would be the best, just a small snack." I answered.

"This is Turkey; you can have whatever you like. We will have some meze sent up to our room and do you know the aniseed drink called raki? Or maybe you prefer wine?" he continued. "Turkey produces some excellent red wines."

I was feeling a lot more relaxed now and comfortable in his presence. My mind was finally at peace. Our hotel room oozed romance and had views across the Bosphorus. As we gazed out at the lights on the passing cargo ships and ferry boats, he turned to me and held me close. "You are beautiful. I am so blessed that you are here with me. We will have an unforgettable holiday together," he said.

Those words meant everything. Those few words had eased all my worries and uncertainties. I was blissfully happy and determined to enjoy this romantic sojourn.

When I emerged from my long hot shower, I felt recharged and revitalised. The soft fluffy hotel bath robe felt comforting against my skin. I felt like a million dollars now.

Placed in front of the hotel room window, was a beautifully crafted timber coffee table and two comfy armchairs. Murat had already ordered up a selection of tasty dips and white cheese and olives. It was exactly what I felt like. He proceeded to pour us each a glass of red wine, and looking intensely into each other's eyes we toasted, 'şerefe.'

Murat had been the perfect gentleman in every way. He had made my arrival so warm and welcoming and I surrendered to his attention. It had been many years since

I had last been fussed over this way. I felt loved and desired. We chatted on through the night, grazing on the mouth-watering meze before us and managing to get through two bottles of wine. It had been a long day but a heavenly start to our reunion. I was yawning more and more now. We had been prolonging the inevitable, both slightly unsure as to how to make the first move. It was time now. Ever so gently and lovingly, Murat took my hand and led me to our bed.

Chapter Fifteen

The road to Cappadocia was glorious. It was freedom. It was a classic road trip through the vividly changing landscapes of Turkey; from the manic traffic of Istanbul to the peaceful plains and villages of central Anatolia. I felt invigorated and enlivened. I hadn't felt this level of happiness for so long. That very part of me had been dormant, but now here I was driving through the Turkish countryside with a caring and passionate man at my side and smiling from ear to ear.

Murat had an eclectic collection of CDs in his glove box and I was in charge of the music. I was his co-pilot, he joked. He soon learnt about my total inability to read maps but I could pick some great tunes. As we drove along we sang at the top of our voices to everything from Tina Turner to the Eagles. We chatted about everything. He loved books and we had read so many of the same novels. He loved the cinema and we chatted about the latest block busters and Oscar winners. We left all the worries about our troubled marriages behind, and indulged ourselves in enjoying these few days together whole heartedly.

The Turkish countryside zoomed past, little villages, mosques and the occasional goat herder tending his flock along the side of the road. There were photo opportunities around every bend and corner. It was all so picturesque and quaint to me. Murat was amused by my desire to photograph a herd of goats or sheep grazing in the pastures, whilst their shepherd relaxed against a tree smoking his cigarette.

"They're just goats," he said.

"But they're Turkish goats," I replied playfully.

We punctuated our trip with short stops at roadhouses where we could visit the bathroom and get a cup of tea. Turkish tea or *çay*, served in little tulip shaped glasses is the mainstay of Turkish life it seemed and we did consume an awful lot of it along the way. Often we were gawked at by the locals, who weren't used to seeing a '*yabanci*' or foreign woman in their town, let alone accompanied by a Turkish man.

"They will have plenty of gossip to take home to their wives tonight," Murat laughed.

We stopped for the night in a little hotel on the other side of Ankara. It was nowhere near as grand as our Istanbul hotel but we were so happy, it didn't matter. We enjoyed our evening stroll around the main square, down the cobbled lanes to the local mosque, and back into the hustle and bustle, where we sat for some dinner and watched the people going about their business. Further along, men were sitting around small tables at the tea shop playing *tavla,* the Turkish name for backgammon. It seemed a very heated game as they were slamming the tiles down and yelling so loud.

"That seems a little aggressive," I said.

Murat just laughed.

"These men have nothing better to do. Probably they are farmers and this is their chill time," he said.

We had passed by many farms where all I saw were the women working in the fields, dressed in their traditional flowery *shalwar* or baggy pants and coloured head scarves. We even saw a group walking along the roadside, obviously going home for the day and the women were lugging all the tools whilst the men strolled along smoking their cigarettes. When these poor women got home, it would then be time for cooking and house work.

"Women still have it quite tough out here," I sighed, trying to imagine their lives.

"Yes, unfortunately my country is still slow when it comes to equality," he said. "We can only hope that change will come soon."

I was hungry to hear more about Turkish life. The *ezan* or call to prayer sounded romantic and exotic to me as it echoed from all the mosques in town. Everything was so vibrant and very different from life in Australia. It felt like I had stepped back in time which seemed appropriate as our first meeting, twenty seven years ago was also a different life time. All those years had gone by and yet here we were today road tripping through Turkey as if we had never been apart.

I felt aglow, this magical interlude, this unexpected affair had brought me back in touch with myself. I started to remember the old Zoe, how I used to feel when every new day was a thrill. I felt noticed, desired and loved. Even my memories of my honeymoon didn't compare to the joy and elation this road trip gave me. Stolen kisses, those little touches, our eyes meeting and the excitement to be back in each other's arms each evening, surely this was heaven.

Murat too was beaming, his smile radiant every time he looked at me, my hand on his knee as we drove on through the vivid landscapes of Anatolia.

As we were getting closer to Cappadocia, neither of us was prepared for the panorama that lay before of us.

Rippling waves of rock against a backdrop of more curving hills and mounds, all bathed in a reddish glow from the slowly setting sun. In the near distance on the right, we could see a rocky outcrop which appeared to have cave homes and a castle on top. Our excitement was mounting as we headed on towards the town of Göreme to reach our cave hotel before night fall.

Terraced above the town and nestled between many huge phallic pillars, we arrived at our destination and marvelled at the magnificent view from the hotel's courtyard. A magical pinkish sky silhouetted the many fairy chimneys before us. As we were being led to our room, we held hands and I felt Murat's grip tighten. I squeezed his arm and looked up to see his smile.

The massive walls of stone contained recessed areas that housed traditional Turkish artefacts such as brass decanters, silver plates, Iznik tile pictures and large candles. The bed was enormous and finished in warm and inviting linens. Antique timber chests served as bedside tables, both topped with tall stemmed brass lamps. Two large timber framed mirrors hung on the walls. Turkish carpets were scattered upon the terracotta tiled floors. We just looked at each other and smiled, reading each other's thoughts and eager to be alone.

This was to be our home, our love nest for the next four nights and it was perfect. We enjoyed late nights out to dinner and lazy mornings in bed. We spent our days touring the area, marvelling at the unique landscape that was Cappadocia. The landscape was like nothing I'd ever seen before, spectacular gorges, undulating hills and these massive phallic pinnacles of rock known as fairy chimneys that dotted the region.

There was certainly no shortage of fascinating activities and excursions to fill our days; from exploring the depths of one of Cappadocia's largest underground cities to hiking through one of the many picturesque valleys. Mother Nature had surely been laughing when she had created the politely named Love Valley. Here, as we ambled along the dirt track passing by these gigantic erotically shaped structures it was impossible not to make the odd joke or comparison to that of an erect penis. The natural erosion of volcanic rock over centuries of time had created this bizarre homage to male fertility. I had never seen anything like it. It had all the makings of an alien landscape, perfect perhaps for the set of a science fiction movie.

Our ramblings brought us to another unique spectacle; the evil eye tree, a tree laden with bright blue glass amulets that twinkled in the sunlight. I had seen these iridescent blue teardrop beads before. In fact, they seemed to be everywhere; a large one adorned the doorway to our hotel room and I had noticed them nailed to the walls in shops and restaurants. When we had visited the Turkish carpet shop and indulged in a glass of *çay* with the owner,

I had noticed a basket full of these talismans near the entrance.

"Don't they look lovely? What are they?" I asked.

"It's just a superstition," Murat replied with a smile. "They are called *nazar boncuğu* and it is thought that they fend off evil spirits and protect the owners from any harm."

"Hmm, nice, I should buy some to take home as gifts," I replied.

Together we gazed silently out past the evil eye tree and over the sprawling landscape before us. Murat put his arm around me and pulled me close. I could sense his solemn mood and suspected he had something to say.

"What are you thinking?" I asked. I already knew the answer.

Murat sighed. "I'm thinking that I don't want these days to end. I'm thinking that I don't want to go back to the troubles awaiting me in Istanbul and I'm thinking that I don't want to be apart from you again."

Chapter Sixteen

We certainly enjoyed our hikes in the valleys and taking in the stunning scenery at ground level, but Cappadocia offered another way to explore and experience the undeniable beauty of its many spectacular valleys. Hot air ballooning was a major attraction here and I was more than keen to give it a go. Of course, to take to the skies in a hot air balloon meant we had to wake up very early in the morning, before sunrise.

"I'm on holiday. I don't want to get up so early," Murat complained.

"But this is a once in a life time opportunity and how romantic," I replied. "Imagine the memory we will create. We can't not go hot air ballooning. We can always go back to bed after," I added with a smile.

On my very first morning in Cappadocia, I had arisen early to visit the bathroom. Before I snuggled back into bed, I had ventured over to our window to take a look at our surroundings. What I saw was awe inspiring and out of this world. The dawn sky was dotted with dozens of brightly coloured balloons drifting along the valley and above the fairy chimneys. They appeared to be suspended in the atmosphere. Each balloon was floating at a different altitude. It looked magical, peaceful and serene. I couldn't help myself. I had to grab my camera and sneak outside to photograph this wonderful sight. It was freezing and my toes felt like ice. Murat was still fast asleep. I dared not disturb him but at least I could show him the photos. I knew it was something I had to do. A hot air balloon ride would be the climax of our sojourn, a memory we would both cherish for ever.

We were picked up from our hotel and taken to the launch site shortly before sunrise. Murat still wasn't convinced that it was worth getting up so early.

"I hope it's worth it," he commented between yawns. "I'm only doing this for you. Hope you will return the favour later," he joked.

The site was a buzz with activity as many brilliantly coloured balloons were laid out on the ground in readiness for inflation. Our balloon was a deep blood red colour with white vertical stripes. In the centre it bore the same white crescent moon and star that is seen on the

Turkish flag. We drank coffee and snacked on biscuits as we watched the activity before us. It was the first time either of us had ever witnessed such a spectacle. Huge fans blew air into the balloon envelope and as flames heated the air, the balloons slowly took shape and rose above the baskets, ready for action.

As soon as our balloon was fully inflated, we were invited to climb aboard the large cane basket and begin our flight over Cappadocia. It was such a strange sensation as our balloon slowly and gracefully rose into the sky. You could hardly feel it moving but a look over the side of the basket, assured us that we were definitely airborne. The sun was rising and the sky was changing colours as we floated up higher and higher. A soft breeze pushed us along as we gazed down upon the villages and homes below; smoke rising from chimneys, dogs barking, children laughing and men preparing for their day at work. It was a surreal experience. We were spectators from above, spying on the life below. Drifting over the township, out over orchards and vineyards and seeing the whole area from a different perspective helped us to realise the vastness of Cappadocia. The air was freezing and we huddled together in the basket, grateful for our big jackets, scarves and gloves. As I looked out over the scene below me, my mind was lost in thought and for a short moment I was in my own world. A gentle squeeze from Murat brought me back to reality.

"How are you feeling?" he asked.

"Overjoyed, happy, blessed, blissful," I replied with a beaming smile. "This is amazing and I will never forget this day."

A year ago I could never have imagined that my life would have taken such a turn and that I would be in the loving arms of another man and holidaying together in Turkey. This was a dream. I was ridiculously happy.

Floating along in silence, except for the intermittent bursts of gas and flames from the burner and the soft whispered comments of our fellow passengers, time seemed to stand still. Everyone was hypnotised by the beauty of what lay below us. Now we were further along the valley and our pilot skilfully and teasingly dipped the balloon down to almost touch the tops of the pinnacles, the fairy chimneys. Other balloons crossed our path and we heard the whoosh as they passed. The panorama from this height was spectacular. A dusting of snow covered some of the taller chimneys. No wonder this was regarded as one of the best ballooning sites in the world. I didn't want it to end but eventually our pilot masterfully and smoothly brought our balloon down to land on the back of a flatbed truck.

We all posed for a souvenir group photo and we toasted this unforgettable occasion with a glass of champagne before heading back to our hotel for breakfast.

Huddled together in the back of the minivan, we were both quiet and deep in thought. Our mood had definitely changed. We both knew that this sweet chapter of our lives was soon coming to an end. We had saved the best for last and now that our hot air ballooning adventure was over, we both knew that soon we would have to return to our former lives.

"But you can stay with me," he said over breakfast. "I will look after you. You don't need to go back to Australia. I'll rent us a house in Istanbul."

"Murat." I softly spoke his name. I didn't know what else to say.

Chapter Seventeen

The long drive back to Istanbul was not as cheerful as our journey to Cappadocia. We would drive straight through, arriving in Istanbul very late and staying the night at Murat's sister's home. He had wanted me to meet his sister and his niece and they were very keen to meet me also.

"*Hoşgeldiniz.* Welcome," she said as she greeted us with smiles and kisses and ushered us into the warmth. Having removed my shoes at the doorway as is customary in a Muslim home, I was promptly given a pair of colourfully embroidered slippers which I politely accepted. Even though it was well past midnight Nihal was awaiting us and had prepared a supper for our arrival. Her daughter, Meryem would also be home soon, she told Murat.

Nihal didn't speak English but that didn't stop her from bombarding Murat with questions, questions about me, I gathered. I was beginning to feel slightly self-conscious as I was aware of her constant gaze. I could see his patience slowly wearing thin as she didn't stop talking and expected him to translate everything she said. He had just driven for over eight hours and was understandably weary, not to mention he had plenty on his mind, as I did.

"She wants to know how our holiday was, and whether you like being in Turkey?" he said. "She also wants to know, what you think of me?" he smiled.

Nihal started again, another rampage of questions. Murat just shook his head and replied to her in Turkish.

"Meryem will be home soon. She speaks English," he sighed with some relief.

Nihal poured us a glass of tea and motioned to us to start eating.

"Please tell her that I am very pleased to meet her and thank her for preparing such an elaborate supper," I said as I sampled the *börek*. It was the perfect comfort food, thin flaky pastry filled with white cheese.

Murat was also hungry and tucked into the freshly made zucchini fritters. I was made to feel very welcome and enjoyed the celebrity status I was given. Murat laughed, "She can't stop staring at you. I don't think she has ever met an Australian before."

Soon we could hear the front door open and watched and waited for Meryem to enter the living room. Of course, Nihal had a lot to say to her daughter first, but then Meryem just smiled and joined us at the table. It sounded like she had been chastised for being out so late.

"Welcome to our home. We have been waiting you," Meryem said. "My mother is cross with me, but this is usual," she said with a grin. "I like to go out with my friends, but she wants me to stay home. Anyway, how was your holiday?"

"Cappadocia was more beautiful than I could have imagined," I replied.

"And my uncle, how is he?" she asked.

"He is very attentive. He took excellent care of me and we had a lovely time," I relied. I really didn't know what to say to that question. I felt that they all had their hearts on me and Murat being a couple.

Murat said something to his niece in Turkish and then Nihal joined in. Whilst they were all deep in conversation, it allowed me some time to look around and take in my surroundings. The flat was modest but warm and homely. I noticed displays of plastic flowers and little statues around the room. Many framed pictures adorned the walls, pictures of their parents and other family members I gathered, possibly a photo of Meryem with Murat's sons.

"Are those your boys with Meryem?" I asked.

"Yes, a couple of years ago. They used to be much closer with Meryem, but since she has started working there isn't the time," he replied.

"And those are your parents?" I asked.

"Yes, again a few years ago. That photo was taken a year before our mother passed," he replied.

"So," said Meryem, eager to get back into the conversation. "For many years we have heard all about you. My uncle talked about you always."

Murat smiled and seemed to cringe slightly.

"Well I had told them all about this beautiful Australian girl I had met in Greece. They loved that story. I showed them photos and so it's like they know you," he said with a smile.

"Yes," said Meryem, "we have photos."

I looked over to Murat, "what photos? From Nafplio?"

"Yes," he replied just as Meryem placed the photos on the table.

"Oh my God," I exclaimed. "I can't believe you still have these after all those years. We both look so young. You look so handsome. What happened?" I joked.

We all laughed and chatted for a while longer till Murat said we need sleep. It had been a very long day and a shower and bed would be heaven.

Nihal took me on a quick tour of her home, showing me the bathroom and what would be our room for the night. Not as romantic as our previous nights, but it felt good to meet Murat's family and to be so warmly welcomed and accepted.

Both Nihal and her daughter Meryem were modern Turkish women. Neither of them wore the head scarf as I had half expected. Instead, they both dressed as any western woman would dress. Like young women all over the globe Meryem enjoyed to go out and have fun with her friends. She had a decent job working for an accountant and she ran her own little car. She was able to help her mother out with the bills and expenses and seemed very mature for her young age. I was glad I had got to meet them both. Their version of Murat's estranged wife helped me to better understand his position and what he had been going through.

"I'm sorry darling, I hope this is okay for you," Murat apologised as we both climbed into the small double bed.

116

"But my sister was so eager to meet you and I wanted you to meet her too."

"Its fine Murat," I insisted. "I am so pleased to meet them too. Tonight I will be asleep before you know it. I'm so weary." I yawned. "You must be exhausted from the drive?"

"Yes I am tired," he muttered "but my heart is heavy at the thought of your leaving."

As tired as we both were, we couldn't sleep. Tomorrow evening I would be flying home to Australia. Murat held me tight in his arms and whispered in my ear, "Please stay with me."

The next morning we woke late, very late. Meryem had already gone off to work. Nihal had prepared breakfast and the table was laid. As she heard us talking, she had begun to brew the coffee over the stove. The aroma was like a wake up call to my senses.

"Coffee's calling," I said as I tried to free myself from Murat's arms. In Turkey, it seemed that traditionally tea was drunk with breakfast but for me I needed my coffee in the morning.

He wrestled me to stay in his embrace. I willingly surrendered.

"Okay, just a little longer," I said as he kissed me. "Nihal is waiting for us. She'll wonder what we are doing."

I would be embarrassed to face her if we didn't get up soon.

"Come on, Murat. I can smell the coffee."

Murat and I had tried to talk last night before sleep. He tried again this morning.

"If you stay, I will rent us a big house," he pleaded again. "I have a decent job and you could teach English. I will help you find a school. There are so many here always looking for native English teachers."

"Murat, I can't stay. I have my son at home and Steve needs to get back to work," I replied. He wasn't being practical. What we just had was like a honeymoon, but now we had to return to reality, the real world.

"Murat, I have had an unforgettable time. I will cherish these days forever. I am so very happy that we have found each other after so many years. It's like a movie, really. I pinch myself to make sure it isn't a dream or my vivid imagination. But Murat I'm sorry, I can't stay. Not this time," I apologized. "We have to be realistic." It was hard for me too, to feel this much love and have to pass it by.

"Maybe when we are both divorced, we can be together, when my son is at university. But at the moment it's just not possible, I'm sorry."

Murat looked so sad and dejected.

Nihal was banging around in the kitchen and mumbling to herself in Turkish.

"Come on, we have to get up," I pressed.

"You go and shower and I'll go and have a coffee with Nihal," I suggested.

I was glad of Nihal's presence as it meant Murat would have to stop pleading with me to stay. I was sad too but I missed Matt and couldn't wait to see him. It's always harder for the one that stays behind. I understood that. But Murat needed to understand that I had responsibilities at home and my son still had another year at school. I would never do anything to sabotage his education and success in his final exams.

"Like?" asked Nihal as she poured me a cup of coffee.

The coffee was strong but just what I needed. I'm sure my spoon would have stood up in it. It definitely woke me up.

As Murat emerged from the bathroom, his sister fired questions at him. With his towel wrapped around his waist and looking extremely sexy, he turned to me.

"Nihal asks if you would like some eggs for breakfast and Turkish sausage."

"That sounds delicious, "I replied.

Breakfast was a banquet. Nihal had been out earlier to get fresh bread. She had homemade butter and fresh honeycomb sent down by family from the Black Sea. She had sliced tomato and cucumber and a variety of cheeses and olives. She had gone all out to impress and our breakfast was a slow and leisurely affair that was as satisfying as any we had tasted at our hotels. To be honest in Cappadocia, we had missed our breakfast two out four times. By the time we rose to start the day, the restaurant was closed and the breakfast dishes had all been cleared away. Still we always managed to find some appetising pastries and tea down town.

Nihal knew we were both sad. She insisted on throwing comments Murat's way but he wasn't in the mood. He snapped at her. His nerves were frayed. Nihal's constant talk was wearying him. He wanted to talk. He wanted to talk to me. He still tried to convince me to stay.

Breakfast was scrumptious but the air between Murat and I was slightly uncomfortable. Nihal had finally stopped talking and we all ate in silence from the vast array of dishes. It was a feast but it did little to bring a smile to Murat's face. Preoccupied and intense, he picked slowly at his eggs. Nihal filled our tea cups and then busied herself in the kitchen, leaving us alone to talk.

"Come on," I said to Murat. "Maybe I can visit again next year, for another short visit, maybe a couple of weeks. What do you think?"

He looked up at me. He had been deep in thought, gazing into his tea cup.

"Of course, any time, you are welcome here. You know I want to spend my life with you," he replied.

This was difficult. I didn't want to think about our final good bye at the airport, our final hug, our final kiss. For me, there was no option, no indecision. I was going home this evening. I had my sons and I had responsibilities at home.

I needed to get organised now and repack my luggage properly. Soon we'd need to make the trip to the airport and I wanted enough time to buy some gifts for the boys. Nihal was clanging dishes in the kitchen, I was gathering together all my stuff in the bedroom and Murat sat quietly at the table, still contemplating his tea.

From one of the neighbouring flats, we could hear the sad and mournful sounds of Turkish art music, a form of traditional music usually listened to over a bottle of raki. One of our evenings in Cappadocia we had spent in a quaint little Anatolian restaurant that had live music. It had been my first taste of the 40% proof aniseed drink and I loved it. Raki is practically the national beverage after tea. It had been an intoxicating evening, for sure. The food was extraordinary and the raki went straight to my head. In front of the tables, on a dimly lit stage, there sat a three piece traditional group, playing this same music.

121

Even though I didn't understand the lyrics, I could feel the mood, the heaviness and sadness. Murat had explained the song to me, adding that most Turkish songs of this style had a similar theme; boy meets girl, they fall in love, for whatever reason they couldn't be together and the boy kills himself.

Well probably fitting music for our situation but hopefully it didn't go that far, I thought.

Chapter Eighteen

Traffic had been as crazy as ever. It was peak time in Istanbul but Murat didn't seem to be flustered. He was used to it, he said. He still wasn't his usual smiley self but we were able to have some light conversation. Mostly, we reminisced about our holiday and magical Cappadocia. We swore that we would return there one day and stay at the same cave hotel. It would now hold a special place in both our hearts.

Murat would start back at work later this evening, and whilst he was in the office, I would be up in the clouds somewhere over eastern Anatolia. I was going home. This whole chapter of my life still seemed surreal to me and now the honeymoon was over, as they say.

When I arrived back in Sydney, Steve and the boys would be meeting me at the airport. We would have a couple hours together with Ben, before Steve, Matt and I would drive the long road north and back to home and my regular life. I had desperately wanted to see Ben and give him his gifts.

My mind was going over everything. Had I remembered my camera, my phone? Did I have my passport and ticket? The kid's presents? What would I buy them? A t-shirt perhaps?

Murat was also going over things. He had by now accepted that I was going home. He was resigned to the fact that nothing could change my mind. Still I could see how much it pained him.

"You have your divorce to get through," I said. "I hope it goes easy for you and not too much stress."

"Hmm," he grunted. "She will want everything. She can have it. I don't care anymore."

I thought about my future. I didn't want to make any waves whilst Matt was still at school. I'd just slip back into my normal routine life and be patient. In the meantime, I could look at getting qualified to teach English. You never know, it could be a new start, a new career. If anything, this sojourn with Murat had given me a new sense of self and a new outlook on my life. I could now envisage my future in colour. I felt empowered and I realised that I wasn't too old for anything. I could do whatever I wanted to and I would start making plans for when Matt leaves for university. I wasn't going to be a sad empty nester or a miserable wife. Murat had given me new hope for my future.

"I will study and get qualified to teach English," I said.

"Yes, you should," he said with a smile. It gave him some hope. "You will have no problem finding a teaching job in Turkey."

"I will come back, Murat. Just you have to wait for me," I added as I squeezed his knee.

As we walked into the departure lounge, suddenly everything and everyone seemed to be moving in slow motion. This was it. This was our goodbye. We had already discussed that we both wanted this to be as least painful as possible. We didn't want to prolong the agony and I didn't want to board my plane sobbing uncontrollably.

"This isn't really goodbye, as I'll see you again soon," I tried to say through my tears. "We won't leave it as long as last time."

"I hope not," he said with a grin. My attempt at a little humour had been rewarded.

"I'll message you when I get home. Okay? Oh and Murat, thank you for an amazing holiday. You have given me precious memories that I will hold onto forever."

Murat was trying hard to hold it all together. His eyes were moist with emotion as he grabbed me and held me tight against him. The airport was as chaotic and noisy as usual but we didn't notice anything except for each other's pain. This was hard.

Finally Murat released me from his grip and wiping his eyes with his sleeve, he turned to walk away.

"Good bye, darling. I'll call you soon. When you are back on your verandah with all the birds," he said as he walked away.

"Bye," I called but he had already left the terminal and I was alone.

My journey home would be a time to collect my thoughts and reminisce on the last week. I was looking forward to seeing my sons. I'd never been away from Matt for so long. I had so much to tell them and experiences to share. I would tell them all about my time in London with Maria; riding the London Eye, the British museum and the iconic British pubs I'd visited. I'd tell them about Berlin and wandering down the famous Kurfürstendamm and the best apple strudel ever.

Then I'd get to my time in Turkey and my travels to Cappadocia. I could tell them about the incredible scenery, the hot air balloon ride and even my cave hotel, but I couldn't tell them about Murat. Not now, not yet.

My Turkish affair was over for now, but it had left me a changed woman. I had gone through a metamorphism. I wasn't the same woman that had left Australia just over two weeks ago. I had rediscovered the old me, the fun me, the 'me' that knew there was a big wide world out there waiting for me and anything was possible.

As my plane took off over Istanbul, I said my goodbyes to Murat and Turkey but I knew in my heart of hearts that I would be back.

☒

PART TWO

Come and Teach

Chapter Nineteen

"You have to be fearless and take chances. Don't live life fearing what comes next. That's not what living is about."

I really wanted to be fearless. I had certainly taken some huge chances. Murat's letter had set this whole ball rolling and now almost two years later to the day, here I was ready to jump in at the deep end. I had left everything I had known, everything that I was familiar with and everyone that I loved and trusted. I had made an epic decision to step, or rather jump, outside of my comfort zone and had accepted an English teaching job in Turkey.

In just a few minutes, I would be standing in front of a class of sixteen Turkish university students, eager to learn English and excited to meet their new English teacher.

"I'm so nervous, I think I'm going to be sick," I said to the Karen, the manager of the English academy in Izmit, Kocaeli.

At fifty one years of age, I was about to embark on my new teaching career. She was well aware of my inexperience. She had interviewed me over skype and I had been perfectly honest about my employment history which certainly did not include teaching.

I had over the previous year attained my TEFL, Teaching English as a Foreign Language certificate; a certificate that qualified me to be an English teacher. However, because I had lived in a rural area of Australia and there were no colleges for this course available to me, my only option was to take an online course. This meant I had no real practical experience.

I had breezed through one hundred and twenty hours of grammar exercises, lesson planning, teaching children, teaching adults, business English, travel English, every type of English teaching that was possible. I had also volunteered at my local adult education centre where we had classes of English for the many new immigrants to our country. I had enjoyed those classes. Usually I was placed with one student and we practised conversation but now here I was, about to step into a classroom with sixteen pairs of eyes upon me.

"Zoe, you'll be fine. We will help you every step of the way. There's nothing to worry about," Karen assured me.

"Oh, I don't know if I can do this," I exclaimed.

My hands were shaking slightly and I felt the warmth in my cheeks.

"Today the students will be more than happy to meet you. I suggest for your first lesson that you tell them a little about yourself and about your life in Australia. Let them ask you questions. And you can also ask them about their lives; what are they studying at university, about their families, their hobbies, etcetera," suggested Karen.

"When writing on the white board, always start on the left side first. And whatever you do, don't tell them that this is your first teaching job," she continued.

"And when you hear the buzzer, it's a ten minute tea break. You can mingle with the students up on the terrace. And remember teachers don't pay for tea."

"Ok, ok I've got it," I said nodding my head and biting my lip.

I was trying to calm myself. It was nearly time for the buzzer to commence lessons. I would give it my best shot. After all, what did I have to lose? Worst case scenario, I'd get the sack on my very first day and I doubted that would happen. These students needed to learn English and I was here to help them. Thankfully, Karen had given me a class of intermediate students first and so communication shouldn't be too bad.

The buzzer screamed down the hallways and students began rushing by and filing into their classrooms. It was show time. One last deep breath and trying to carry myself with confidence, I walked calmly into my classroom.

All the noise and chatter faded and suddenly all eyes were focused attentively on me. With a big smile and hopefully radiating my friendliness, I began the first class of my English teaching career.

"Good morning, students. My name is Zoe. I am from Australia, and I am your teacher for this course of English."

Chapter Twenty

It had been a long but busy year since my sojourn with Murat in Cappadocia.

On my return to Australia, I had wasted no time finding a course for preparing to teach English. Matt was now in his final year of school and together we conquered all the stresses that it entailed. We were both focused on our studies and life moved along smoothly. Steve continued to return home for the odd weekend and as usual I just tried to get through it and breathed a sigh of relief as his car finally pulled out of the driveway again.

Murat and I had continued to communicate every way we could. I always looked forward to his daily calls and his funny text messages. We shared our day's events and everything else that was happening in our lives. Although many kilometres separated us, we were close.

The biggest development was the complete turnaround of his wife now and her refusal to go through with the divorce. After she had thrown him out of their family home and gone to the courts to set a divorce date, she now begged him to come home. One of Murat's best friends, who he had confided in and thought he could trust, had taken the news of our affair straight to Asli and that had changed everything. If another woman wanted her man, she reasoned, surely he must be worth keeping. She didn't, however, change her nasty ways or her aggression. She told all their neighbours that Murat had cheated on her and so whenever he returned home to see his sons, he was faced with their scorn and disdain. She constantly called him at work and most of his work colleagues were on Asli's side. Even his long-time friends had deserted him. Murat's life was now a living hell.

As is usual in Turkish culture, she had called together all the family members from both sides for an intervention. His father was too old and frail to travel now but his uncles and his brother travelled down from the Black Sea. All of her family were present. She even summoned Murat's manager to join them. I couldn't fathom such interference. Murat's sister Nihal would have nothing to do with it.

It was a heart wrenching afternoon, when he was questioned and interrogated about his relationship with the Australian woman.

"They wanted to know everything about you," he said. "They wanted to know how we met and how we got in contact. They don't understand how life with Asli is. She's a monster and I can't live with her anymore. I wish you were here, I need you," he pleaded.

All I could do was listen patiently and try to console him. It was hard to fathom how many people got involved in this relationship issue that should be between a man and his wife. This wasn't about love. This was more about logistics and money. This was Turkey.

"Well, they can't force you to stay with her, can they?" I questioned.

"They can make my life hell. She's threatening to keep my sons away from me. She says that they will disown me if I don't come back."

"Well then Murat, I think you need to go back to her." I said. "It seems they have all ganged up on you and made you out to be the bad one. I'm so sorry for you. I hate that you're going through all of this because of me."

Murat sighed. "I hate this too and I hate her more than ever. I just want to be with you. Come to me. Come and teach English."

Often our chats ended on this sad note and my nights were sleepless. I felt like the villain that had caused all this trouble, but then again it was he who had first contacted me.

"He started it'" said Cheryl, always the good friend. "I mean you were both separated and so you have done nothing wrong. Not to mention that you held off for so long before you even told him about your marriage situation. It's sad what has happened but it's not your fault"

"Yes, it is very sad," I replied. "I think I need to walk away from this. Turkish culture isn't something I want to mess with. I'd hate for his sons to disown him."

As the year progressed, Murat's situation flowed through troughs and crests. I really was so far removed from the problem that I had to leave it in his hands and hope he made the best decision for himself. I was prepared for the fact that most likely our relationship would be over. But no, he wouldn't have it.

"No," he protested. "I will not bow to their commands. Our marriage is over. She wanted the divorce and now she changes her mind. It's not right. I'll give her whatever she wants, but I want to be with you."

"How's your course going, by the way?" he inquired.

"Good. Nearly finished actually. Soon I'll be a fully qualified English teacher. A new qualification is always a bonus on the resume. Even if I don't ever teach English, I've learnt a new skill." I replied.

"Why will you never teach English?" he questioned. "Zoe, I still want you to come to Turkey. I want you here with me. Nothing's changed."

"Everything's changed." I exclaimed. "I don't want to be the one that breaks up your marriage. I don't want to be the one that causes you to lose your sons."

"Zoe, please don't talk that way. I can't be with her anymore. You heard my sister. She told you how bad my situation was. No, nothing has changed, Zoe. We will still be together. I promise you."

"Ok, we'll see. We still have a few months before Matt finishes school and graduates. And then I have to find a job. That could take a while. So, we'll just wait and see. Whatever will be, will be," I said philosophically.

The months were flying by and the year was coming to an end. My course was finished and I had received my certificate of completion. Matt was finishing up his exams and I was looking forward to the day that he could just relax, sleep in, take a dip in the pool and watch as much television as he wanted.

Though not convinced about the future of my relationship with Murat now, I still knew that I was ready to take a plunge into life; to step outside of my comfort zone and try something different. I had read all the self-help books and felt empowered. I wasn't going to be an empty nester. And I certainly wasn't going to be sitting here waiting for Steve's weekend visits which I dreaded. I was ready to take on the world and find my way into a new life.

I had been researching on the internet about teaching English overseas. People's accounts of their experiences were encouraging and even inspirational. There seemed to be a heap of jobs on offer in China but with the overpopulation and thick pollution, China didn't appeal to me. Turkey did appeal. I had loved it there. It was exotic and colourful. Yes, Murat was there and that's how this whole thing had started but perhaps I needed to cut Murat free.

"Maybe I don't love Murat as much as he loves me," I confided in Cheryl. "Maybe I was in love with the excitement and adventure of it all."

"Hmm, maybe that's true. He did make you very happy and you were definitely a changed person. It was good to see you smiling," she replied. "But perhaps it was the excitement of it all and the break from routine."

I had to agree. Just lately I had been questioning my love. Did I love him? Or did I love how he made me feel? I think it was the latter. And now that this situation with his wife had arisen, I wasn't sure I wanted any part of it. I sounded cold and heartless but to be completely honest, I think it was the affair, the secrecy and romance of travelling to a foreign country that I had been in love with. I didn't know how I really felt. I was torn. Of course, I did love him in some way. We certainly got on well. He was definitely attractive to me. I pictured his face; his deep brown eyes, his two day growth speckled with grey and his wide smile. I visualised his body; his flawless olive skin and his strong smooth chest where I would rest my head and find comfort in the gentle pulse of his heart beat. Yes, I did love him but …something was missing. I just couldn't put a finger on it.

Why had he come back into my life after all those years? Almost twenty seven years later. That was fate, for sure. At one point I was feeling so low and at forty nine years old, I felt my life was over. My kids wouldn't need me for much longer and my marriage was in a dismal state. I was dreading my fiftieth birthday. I had no direction and didn't see beyond my immediate surroundings.

Murat's letter had definitely changed all that. Yes, I would always have to accredit him for the life changes I made because he showed me that I wasn't too old and that there was a whole world out there just waiting for me to explore. He empowered me and I felt invincible. Yes, I would always be indebted to Murat for that. His love had brought me back to life.

Chapter Twenty One

At the time, the end of 2008, Turkey was definitely
going through a boom time for English. The business of
teaching English was absolutely flourishing and it seemed
that Turkey was positively embracing the English
language and realising the importance of English for their
future employment opportunities, business, education
and travel. There had been a program to teach English in
the schools but the Turkish English teachers just weren't
doing a good enough job and that's where the
opportunities for native English speakers were becoming
more abundant and quite well paid.

The idea of teaching English wasn't entirely new to me.
I had read about it and the various courses to qualify as an
English teacher many years before this recent reunion
with Murat. It had always appealed to me and I had
gathered a collection of articles and pamphlets about it

but the timing was never right. I had a family to care for, children to run around to their after school activities and a massive garden to keep under control. I was also working three days a week and the weekends were manic with soccer or junior life saving. Of course, it wasn't my time and all those pamphlets about teaching English as a foreign language were stored down beneath the books and magazines in my bedside table.

But now, with Ben already at university in Sydney and Matt on the very brink of finishing high school and also going to university, my time didn't seem too far away. Whereas before I had no direction about my life after Matt left, now I had this whole new world of English teaching to explore. It was beckoning me. With Murat or without Murat, I still felt drawn to Turkey. I had loved everything about Turkey when I first visited there in 1985, touring by motorbike with Steve and I loved it last year, visiting Cappadocia with Murat. It was definitely a country of contrasts, colour, excitement, history, hospitable people and delicious food. It ticked all the boxes for me and I had decided that it would be my Turkish adventure.

One day as I was surfing the net, I came across a forum for women travellers and you could request to have a female mentor in your chosen city. I did have Murat to answer all my questions and he did want so desperately to help me in every way. But still I felt that the opinions and views of another foreign woman in Istanbul would be helpful and perhaps shine a different light on things. I signed up and requested a mentor in Istanbul and that's how I met Sue.

Sue was British, my age and taught English in an academy in a small city called Adapazari, about two hours out of Istanbul. She was very friendly and obviously loved what she did. We began chatting on Skype and I was inspired by her stories of life in Turkey. Reading some reviews on the internet, they had talked about schools and academies that didn't pay their employees, didn't turn on the heating in winter, sleazy managers and terrible working conditions. Sue's experience was nothing like that. She worked in a modern academy that provided all text books and teaching aids. She was provided with a comfortable furnished studio apartment just minutes away from her academy and her manager was sympathetic and understanding when she had to make an emergency trip home to see her mum who had taken a serious fall. It was all positive. That's what I needed to hear. I felt even more encouraged and inspired. This would be my new path. A new chapter of my life.

"They are advertising for native English teachers in Izmit, Kocaeli. They are quite desperate I think and will pay well," Sue said. "Izmit is about an hour from me. We could meet up regularly for lunch dates," she encouraged.

This was my chance. I needed to submit an application. I did really want this but a small part of me hoped they wouldn't contact me. I was scared. Was I crazy? Was moving to Turkey a crazy idea? I consoled myself with the realisation that I already had a support system. I had Murat and now I had Sue. I had people who would help through any hurdles and hoops I needed to jump.

Matt was my rock. I told him about the job opportunity in Izmit and he was all for it.

"Do it, mum," he encouraged, "even if it's just for six months. It would be an awesome experience."

He was right. I would apply.

Matt was waiting on his results and which university he would be accepted into. We both knew that he would get his first choice and that would be the same university in Sydney where his brother was studying. Ben had made university life sound so amazing; all the parties and concerts, outings and excursions, rock climbing and sailing, campus life sounded like one big party. It must have been good because it was difficult these days to get him to come home for a weekend. Of course, there was the new girlfriend and girlfriends always trump mother.

Matt was looking forward to joining Ben and living on campus but he was also toying with the idea of a gap year. We had discussed the pros and cons of a gap year many times. Ben had taken a gap year and we saw how beneficial it had been. He had time to think about his future and what career path he wanted to follow and had in the end changed his degree choice. I could only see the benefits really. In his gap year, Ben had worked and travelled and definitely grown through these experiences. I was keen for Matt to have the same.

"What about if I get a job in Turkey, you come over with me?" I suggested. "It would be fantastic for me and a great opportunity for you, your gap year. What do you think?"

"Cool. I think that would be super awesome," he replied.

"Well, let's work towards that. First I need to get a job," I exclaimed. My insides were jumping. We hugged. This would be an adventure for us both.

When the email arrived from the English academy in Izmit, I just stared at it for a while, trying to process what this could mean. Part of me hoped it was an offer for an interview and another part of me hoped it was a polite rejection. I could hear Matt playing guitar in his bedroom.

"Matt, I got a reply to my application," I called.

"Huh? What did you say?" Matt had now joined me.

"I have a reply from the English academy in Turkey."

"What do they say?" he asked.

"I don't know. I haven't opened it yet. I'm scared," I replied sheepishly.

"Mum, open it," he ordered.

"I can't believe it. They want to interview me," I screamed.

I grabbed Matt and kissed him on the cheek.

"An interview tomorrow via Skype," I added. "Gosh, this is getting too real. We might be going to Turkey."

I needed a chardonnay and I offered Matt a small one to celebrate what might be the start of our epic Turkish adventure. I couldn't wait to tell Murat. He would be very impressed with me, for sure.

I had the interview and the job offer. It was all happening too fast. It was exciting but many nights I lay in bed going through various scenarios, dreaming up every possible thing that could wrong and questioning my decision to accept. I had signed and returned the contract, but surely they couldn't hold me to that. After all I was in Australia. What could they do? Then again, maybe this was the perfect opportunity.

Chapter Twenty Two

'Congratulations,' said Murat. 'This is wonderful news. When do you start?'

"I plan to leave here the day after Christmas and I will start teaching early in the new year. I can't believe this is happening," I replied. "I need to organise my airfare and get things in order here."

Gosh, I need to tell Steve, I thought. That will be a shock to his system, especially when he hears that Matt is going to join me for his gap year. My head was an utter mishmash of thoughts and ideas.

Matt and I had been eagerly working out our plans. He had a summer job and didn't want to leave before the school holidays were over, so we planned that he would join me two months later. That gave me enough time to settle in and find us a flat. It would also give me time to see where my relationship with Murat was heading before I even broached the topic with Matt.

"Someone from the academy will meet me at the airport and take me to the staff housing, where I can stay for up to three months," I explained to Murat.

"No way," he replied. "I will meet you at the airport and we will have a couple days together and then I will take you to Izmit."

"Hmm, I guess that could work. I'll need to tell Karen at the academy about this change to the plans. I'm sure she'll be fine with it."

Sue in Adapazari was excited and we had already made a future lunch date. Cheryl was excited and couldn't believe how brave I was.

"Wow, you are a changed person these days," she declared. "Aren't you a little scared?"

"I'm terrified," I replied with a laugh.

All this excitement made me feel alive with a purpose, a new purpose, a new stage of my life. The knowledge that Matt was joining me also gave me a sense of security and besides if we didn't like it we could come home.

Steve was making one of his weekend visits and Matt and I thought it was the perfect time to break this monumental news to him.

We took our seats at our favourite Thai restaurant. Matt was bubbling with excitement and Steve could tell that something was up. As Steve poured me a glass of much needed chardonnay, I felt the time was fitting to begin this conversation. Matt's smiling and excitement was contagious and I couldn't keep a straight face either.

"What are you two up to?" inquired Steve. "Matt's got ants in his pants or something."

"Well, we have some news; big news, really big news actually. I have been offered a new job and I have accepted the position." I explained, trying to keep a serious face.

"In Turkey," blurted Matt. He just couldn't keep it in anymore.

"Turkey? Istanbul, Turkey?" Steve was confused.

"Yes. Turkey. I'm going to teach English in a language academy in Izmit, about an hour from Istanbul," I explained.

"And I'm going too," blurted Matt with a smile from ear to ear.

Clearly, this was a lot for Steve to absorb. He gulped his wine.

"You're going too?" he aimed at Matt.

"Ok, I got a job teaching English and Matt will join me for his gap year. It's a wonderful opportunity for him, don't you think?" I asked.

"Well sure, it is. It's a bit sudden and I just need a moment to process this all."

As our food arrived at the table, we began to quietly sample the delicious Thai cuisine. We were all deep in thought as we focused on the food before us.

"When do you leave?" enquired Steve finally.

"Just after Christmas and Matt's going to join me end of February," I replied. "That gives me enough time to sort out a flat for us."

"Hmm, yes," Steve nodded as he took another serving of the special Thai fried rice. "Well I never could have imagined this sort of news, but I knew something was brewing by the way Matt kept smiling and fidgeting all day."

"Have you researched Izmit?" he asked.

"Sure. Actually you might remember the devastating earthquake of 1999? Remember we were in Paris at the time? It was on all the news. Well, Izmit was very close to the epicentre," I explained. "As you can imagine, much of the city was destroyed and so there has been a lot of rebuilding and modernisation since. The death toll was over twenty thousand people. It was a major catastrophe."

"Right, I remember. Oh aren't you scared of another earthquake?" he asked.

"They predict another one in ten years or so, but I think we're safe for the meantime, but I guess you can never really tell," I replied.

I felt that dinner had gone well and Steve had taken the news quite pleasantly. From here on in, it would be organising Matt's and my flights and trying to find a warm winter jacket, which in summer in sub-tropical Australia was probably going to be my biggest challenge.

As the days passed and my departure day was fast approaching, Matt and I were getting more and more excited. It was really happening. We were going to Turkey.

Chapter Twenty Three

As I walked out through the exit gates of Istanbul's
Atatürk airport a strong sense of *deja vu* fell upon me. It
had been just over a year since I had last walked this path.
I could remember how scared and anxious I had been,
taking refuge at the Gloria Jeans coffee shop whilst I
waited for Murat to meet me. It had been our first
reunion after twenty seven years, so of course I was
anxious.

Today, I was a much more self-assured woman and the
crowds and chaos didn't seem to unnerve me in any way. I
confidently pushed my way through the throng of people
and made my way to the same seat at the same Gloria
Jeans coffee shop. I couldn't help but smile and think to
myself just how much my life has changed in the last two
years. Here I was today, in Turkey and about to embark
on a new life and a totally new career as an English

teacher. I was proud of myself. Who says women in their fifties can't do anything? We can do everything. Fifty is the new thirty. I'd recently read that in a magazine and now I felt I was living proof.

Murat was late again but after some fifteen minutes and a couple of text messages, there he was, walking through the doors and looking as handsome as ever. His smile radiated across his face as he rushed towards me and took me in his arms. It was amazing to see him again. I felt overwhelmed with emotion and warm and comforted in his embrace. I didn't want him to release me.

"My darling, you are here again," he said. "I'm so proud of you. You have a new job. It's incredible news."

"Yes, I'm here again. I can't quite believe it."

"So, I have booked our hotel for tonight. Nihal and Meryem send their love and hope to see you soon. I told them that you can visit any weekend as it's only an hour on the bus from Izmit to Istanbul."

"Oh, that's great. I'd love to visit them. They can teach me some Turkish," I replied.

It felt good to know that I had friends and people around me that I could visit and call on if I needed help. So far, no mention of Murat's wife and the developments in that situation but I knew that at some point soon, it would need to be discussed. If she knew that I was in

153

Turkey, it may cause more grief and even give her more reason to be aggressive.

I had personally felt her aggression now. A few weeks ago I had received a couple of very malicious and vitriolic text messages from her. She had somehow found the opportunity to get into Murat's phone and found messages from me. She had my number now and didn't refrain from using it. Of course, I just ignored them but they had made me feel like the villain and made me feel dirty. I had shared this with Murat and he had insisted that I just ignore her.

"She's like a fox," he said. "She is cunning and sneaky. She has a friend on the fifth floor of our flats that speaks English and she has been helping her. She's crazy. Just ignore her."

"Murat, that's easy for you to say but it made me feel cheap." I said. "And how did she get your phone? You need to be more vigilant."

"Yes, I agree," he replied. "As I said, she is so cunning. I'm sorry darling. She has also been sending bad texts to Nihal and Meryem. She's crazy, we say *deli*. Anyway darling, can we just enjoy our night and forget all about her and these problems? I've missed you so much."

****

All couples have their moments, their little disagreements but so far, for Murat and me it had been clear sailing. Long distance relationships are always difficult. Well admittedly, this was my first long distance relationship but I had to agree with everything I'd ever read or heard about this topic. It is difficult. At times you just want to reach through the phone to touch the other person. You yearn to be held, to be kissed. You miss the passion. You want to console your partner through the hard times and you want to celebrate with them for the good times.

Murat and I had been communicating long distance for two years now. We talked or messaged almost daily. Gosh, more than I ever talked or messaged with Steve. We knew everything about each other and our daily routines. In some ways our long distance communication had brought us closer. I can't even recall ever really having any sort of disagreement. We were tight. We were in harmony.

On our trip to Cappadocia last year, I had at times noticed some little quirks. There were moments when I was stopped in my tracks and needed to assess the situation. There were the times when Murat took it upon himself to order my meal for me. I mean, the waiter would give us both a menu and then return to take our order. Without even consulting with me, Murat would rattle off his selection in Turkish and the waiter would leave.

"I haven't ordered yet," I would say.

155

"I ordered for you, darling," Murat would say.

I would protest and he would defend himself by saying that he wanted me to sample the very best of Turkish cuisine and that he knew what I liked.

I would say something like, "I'm not your Turkish wife. I'm an Australian woman and I order for myself."

He would apologize and say that he meant nothing by it and I would accept his apology. In some strange way I enjoyed his taking command of situations but it had a limit. Being a strong, independent Australian woman I wasn't to be controlled or bossed around, unless I wanted too.

"Tomorrow I will take you to Izmit and I will come with you to the academy," Murat announced.

"That's really nice of you to drive me to Izmit, Murat but you don't need to come to the academy," I replied.

"Of course, I do," he replied. "I need to speak with the manager and check that everything is fine."

"You are not going to speak with my manager, Murat," I responded, feeling the heat rising to my cheeks. "This is my job. I'm perfectly capable of going in on my own and if I encounter any problems, I'll just leave."

"Darling, I just want to talk to him and see that they look after you. I'm just thinking of you."

"First of all, the manager is a woman. Her name is Karen and she's from the United States. I think I can trust her. I really don't need you to interrogate her and embarrass me. I can look after myself, thank you." I replied.

"Ok, but I just want to look after you and make sure you are safe."

"Thank you Murat, but I'll be fine. I'll message you in the evening and let you know everything that's happened. I hope to organise a Turkish phone soon so I might be able to call you."

"Ok," Murat replied. He seemed despondent now.

"Are you Ok?" I asked. "Murat, I think this is an example of our cultural differences. In the west, women are strong and we can organise ourselves. It's lovely that you want to take care of me, but some things I'm perfectly capable of doing by myself. Don't be upset with me now."

"Ok."

"Plus, I don't want everyone to know about my private life," I added.

"Ok."

Murat was staring at the television in our room and ignoring me now. He was hurt and trying to understand my reasoning.

"So tell me about the situation with Asli and your divorce," I asked, trying to change the subject.

"What divorce? She is refusing to divorce me now. All the family are on my back and it's a nightmare," he replied. "I really don't know my options. Besides my sister and niece, everyone else is against me."

"Oh, I'm sorry to hear that. What will you do?" I asked.

"I will continue to live at my sister's home and see what arrangements Asli and I can come to. I still fully support her and the boys. She always calls for more money. She says if we do divorce she will take everything. She can have the house. I don't want it."

The stress was taking its toll on Murat and he wasn't sleeping well. He worked the night shifts and then couldn't sleep through the day. He had started to smoke again, just an occasional cigarette he said, and I was sure he was drinking more than usual.

Despite our first solid disagreement, we enjoyed our time together in our special hotel. It had been over a year since we had last been together and so we had a lot of catching up to do. I knew that Murat just wanted to take care of me, but the thought of him taking me to the academy like a parent taking their child to kindergarten absolutely freaked me out. Maybe I had over reacted but I needed to set the boundaries and my job was my job.

Going over all these little things in my mind, I eventually drifted off to sleep in his arms, feeling warm and loved.

From the terrace we could see over the Gulf of Izmit that was part of the Sea of Marmara and lead down to Istanbul and the Black Sea. Karen explained that Izmit was an important industrial city with an oil refinery and paper and cement factories.

"Most of our students are from the local Kocaeli University. Its main department is engineering. We also get some already qualified engineers from the Ford Motor Company which is also located here in Izmit," she said.

"You'll find that all the students are very respectful and eager to learn. I really think that you will enjoy it here, Zoe. We have fifteen native English speakers teaching here so you won't be lonely. There is always something going on and you'll find that the students will love to hang out with you after class too," she continued.

"Along the waterfront you'll find a well-kept park area with lots of bars and restaurants. It's very pleasant. I've been living here in Izmit for about five years now and before that I lived in Istanbul for twelve years. I love living in Turkey. I go back to the States very year or so for a holiday but I'm always happy to return to Turkey."

Hearing all about Izmit and about Karen's life in Turkey made me excited and happy with my decision to come here. I explained to Karen that my son would be joining me in a couple of months.

"That will be wonderful for our students to meet a young Australian guy. He will have many friends here, I'm sure," she said. "We might even get him teaching," she said with a giggle.

Everything was perfect and I felt completely at ease now. The only other thing I wondered about was the staff housing and where I would be sleeping this night.

"Ok, I will take you out to the staff house shortly. Unfortunately, it's a bit far out of the city and you'll need to take a bus but I'll show you where the bus stop is and what to say. Don't worry, we'll look after you."

Karen had made a great first impression and in a small way, I felt a part of the school team already and I looked forward to meeting the other teachers. I think when anyone moves to a foreign country to start a new job, it's a blessing to get that kind of support right from the word go.

"Tomorrow night we are having a welcoming dinner for you and Angie, the other newbie, and you'll get to meet everyone. You'll meet Angie tonight as she's out at the staff housing. It's just the two of you out there at the moment. Angie's from the States, but we do have another Australian teacher on the staff. You'll meet him tomorrow."

"It all sounds great," I replied. "I'll be looking at getting my own flat before my son arrives."

"And we'll help you with that. You'll also receive a renting allowance on top of your pay, so we have you covered."

As we drove out of town I began to notice snow on the hills. We were heading to a small rural town called Yuvacik. I couldn't help myself from smiling. I was in Turkey. It was all feeling very real now.

We drove for about thirty minutes, briefly stopping to buy me some bed linen and a cheap phone and Turkish sim card. I was surprised at just how modern the shopping centre was. Turkey was certainly a country of contrasts.

"This is the bus stop. You will take bus number three. And there is your new home," she said pointing to a large modern block of apartments.

The apartment was warm but very sparsely furnished. The kitchen seemed adequate, as did the bathroom but my room was a mattress on the floor, not quite what I had expected. Well I guess it will do for a short time.

"Yeah, not too comfortable but at least it's warm and it has strong Wi-Fi," Karen said with a smile.

"All part of the adventure," I replied.

"Most teachers do move into their own furnished flats reasonably soon. This is just a temporary place," she added.

"Yep," I agreed.

"Ok, I'll leave you to get organised. So tomorrow you can come to school if you like or just relax. We'll see you at dinner tomorrow night and I think there are plans for New Year's Eve celebrations on Saturday also," she said as she left.

I was alone; in a foreign flat, in a foreign country, a long way from home. I felt slightly at a loss for what to do next. I gazed aimlessly out of the window. The distant mountains were covered with snow. It looked magic. The surrounding houses all had lovely large gardens and small green houses. Thick grey swirls rose from their chimneys and the sky was heavy was the smoke. My room was toasty warm from the radiator under my window and I was grateful for that.

Maybe I should call Murat, I thought. I could give him my new number and let him know I was safe and warm in the staff housing. He's probably waiting to hear from me, I thought. I need to call Matt too on Skype. Need to work out the time difference.

"*Efendim*," he answered.

"Hello. It's me. This is my new number," I said.

"Oh Zoe, great. So how is it?"

"It's ok," I replied and proceeded to tell him everything about the school and the flat.

"Tomorrow there is a welcoming dinner for me and the other new teacher," I added. "I won't start teaching till after the New Year."

"My sister has invited you to her home for the weekend to celebrate the New Year together. I will be working but will see you in the morning," he said.

"Um, Saturday there is a New Year celebration here too. I think it is important to be social with the other teachers, don't you?" I asked

"Zoe, I prefer that you go to Nihal's home. She will prepare some special food in your honour," he added.

I felt he was pressuring me and I didn't like it.

"Let me see how tomorrow night's welcome dinner works out. I will get to meet all the other foreign teachers and that will give me some idea about how I will spend the New Year. Ok?"

"So I'll tell Nihal that you will come?" he asked again.

"I'm not sure Murat. Let me tell you tomorrow." I replied.

"She is expecting you," he continued.

I didn't like this kind of pressure.

"Ok, I have to go now. Bye," I ended our conversation before I said something I would regret.

At that same moment the front door opened and in marched Angie.

"Freezing out there," she said. "Hi. I'm Angie."

"Hi, I'm Zoe."

"You just get in?" she asked.

"Yeah. And you?"

"I've been here a couple of days. Glad to have some company now. It's been a bit lonely out here. I've been exploring the city centre and just chilling. Apparently, we won't start lessons until after the New Year. Is that what Karen told you?" she asked.

"Yes and she also said that there is a welcoming dinner in our honour tomorrow evening so that we can meet the other teachers," I replied.

"Yes. That should be fun. Do you fancy going out and getting some dinner now? There's a decent restaurant just near the bus stop. I've had a couple meals there and they've been really good."

As there was no food in the house, that did seem like an excellent idea. I'd enjoyed a big Turkish breakfast with Murat but that was quite a few hours ago. Now that I thought about it, I was very hungry.

Together we headed out into the icy cold air, rugged up as best as we could and made our way to the small restaurant across the way. It felt funny for me to be wearing gloves and scarves and heavy jackets. Well actually, my jacket wasn't so heavy, but it was the best I could find at the time. I still needed to go and do some proper cold weather clothes shopping, but for the meantime layers were doing the trick. At home in winter, the most we ever needed was a jumper. The boys still wore shorts to school in the winter. But here it was icy cold and it could even snow tonight, Karen had said. That was exciting for me.

The atmosphere inside the restaurant was warm and inviting and we were ushered to a table by the radiator and given the menus. Of course, the menus were all in Turkish so this was a challenge but with the waiter's small knowledge of English we managed to select a few dishes that did sound delicious.

We chatted on through the evening, sharing our stories as travellers often do and why we came to Turkey to teach English. Angie was from Washington, a retired bank teller and new to teaching like me. She had also just wanted a change but the more I learnt about Angie, I soon realised that she seemed slightly obsessed with her religion. All of her exploring in Izmit had been trying to find a Christian church, which I found rather strange as she had elected to come to an Islamic country.

"So I've been told I can find a Christian church in Istanbul, but not in Izmit," she explained.

"Ok. You do know that Turkey is an Islamic country?" I remarked.

I really couldn't understand why you would come to an Islamic country if praying in a church was so important to you, but each to their own, I guess. I enjoyed my dinner with a few wines and the conversation was flowing easily when my phone buzzed; my first call on my new phone and of course, it was Murat.

"*Merhaba*. How are you, my darling," he asked.

"I'm great. Just out to dinner with the other new teacher," I replied.

"But darling, it's late now. You should be at home. Who is this other teacher? Man or woman?" he asked.

"Angie, she is from America. And yes, we are going home shortly," I replied.

Was he interrogating me?

"Ok, you shouldn't be out alone so late at night. Go home now, please and call me when you get home."

"Murat, I'm not alone. I'm with Angie. We'll go home soon, when we've finished our wine."

"You're drinking alcohol?"

"Yes, Murat. We are sharing a bottle of your delicious Turkish red wine."

His questions and controlling ways were beginning to get to me. My blood was boiling. I wasn't going to stand for this. Who did he think he was?

"Good night, Murat."

I was fuming and Angie could see it. I felt lucky that our call hadn't ended in an argument but really this kind of controlling behaviour needed to stop. I felt like he didn't trust me. I was going to have to have a chat with him about this. And, as for the New Year's Eve celebrations, I was quite certain now that I was going to party with the teachers. His sister Nihal was lovely and we got on very well but we did have a language problem and just sitting in her flat didn't really sound like a fun New Year's Eve. I could visit her the weekend after. He was going to be mad. I knew that for sure. I hadn't seen this side of Murat before. It was certainly a shock to me.

Chapter Twenty Four

Through the night there had been a heavy snowfall. As there was only a thin sheet hanging over my window, I was awoken by the strange light. The night sky was a luminous pink colour and as I went to my window to investigate I saw a constant stream of snowflakes falling to earth and covering the ground with a thick carpet. Where I lived in sub-tropical Australia, of course we never saw snow, so this was quite a memorable spectacle for me. It was magical. In the morning I gazed out of my window again to see the fields and footpaths thickly covered and speckled with the many footprints of the children as they went to school. I was looking forward to going out into this winter wonderland.

About midmorning, Angie and I took the bus into town. I enjoyed the bus trip as it wound its way through the little villages and farmland down the mountain and eventually dropping us off on the side of the busy expressway. Izmit hadn't had the snowfall that we had experienced up at Yuvacik. Izmit was just cold and grey.

Climbing the stairs of a huge overpass, we were thrust into the colourful and chaotic streets of the city centre. Vendors with their trolleys selling the delicious sesame seed encrusted pretzel like breads called at the top of their voices; *simit, simit.*

They did look inviting and we succumbed to one seller's beckoning call. It was warm and satisfying on this fresh icy morning. I needed coffee now. Our academy was in a large square modern looking building not far from the overpass. It took over three floors but on the ground floor was a coffee shop, *Kahve Dunyasi*, a Turkish version of Starbucks; maybe even better than Starbucks. It had a magnificent selection of cakes and chocolates on display and when you ordered a coffee you got a solid chocolate teaspoon on your saucer. The cakes were really to die for. You could sit inside or outside there were gas furnaces and small blankets on every chair.

The smokers, of course, preferred to sit outside. I had never seen so many people smoking. In Australia smoking was practically a social taboo but here in Turkey it was a favourite and very popular indulgence. I didn't mind too much and the thought occurred to me that perhaps I would succumb to this bad habit also. I had smoked a little in my twenties but since then I had never even given it a thought. Now it was going to be hard to resist as everyone smoked and everyone generously offered out their cigarettes. Despite the smoking, the coffee was the best, the seating was comfortable and I really like this place. It was an obvious favourite with all the teachers due to its convenient location and soon I too would be stopping there regularly before and after classes for my caffeine fix and chocolate teaspoon.

There were two Starbucks in Izmit and the one on the main street was another popular meeting spot for all the foreigners in town, which included teachers from the other academies and schools. At any time of day, you would see them sitting in the comfy armchairs with their laptops open and doing some work or even skyping with their family and friends back home. I too, became a regular patron of Starbucks and often filled some hours sitting in there between classes. There was always someone around to chat with. Often, I would meet students there for some English practice. I never charged but I know that other teachers did. I got enough satisfaction from just knowing that I was helping in some small way.

Angie and I spent our day exploring Izmit and getting familiar with our surroundings. We popped in to see Karen at the academy and had another coffee up on the terrace. Karen offered us the opportunity to sit in on a class in progress and I found this a big confidence boost.

It wasn't going to be too bad. The teacher giving the class was actually from Vietnam and her English wasn't perfect but I wasn't going to highlight any of her mistakes. It did make me think however, how lucky I was to be born in an English speaking country. English was the language of the world and I was fortunate enough that this skill could provide me with a new career and income. I was determined to give it my best and be of any assistance to anyone who wanted to learn my language. Also, I thought that I would try my best to learn some Turkish, at least the greetings and pleasantries.

Murat's call came just as we were making our way with Karen to the restaurant for our welcoming dinner.

"Hi Murat," I answered.

"Hello, my darling. How was your day?" he asked.

"Great. Actually we are just about to go to dinner now. Remember I told you? Our welcoming dinner? To meet all the other teachers that work here."

"Oh. You are having such a social life now, Zoe. What time will you be home?" he asked.

"I don't know what time this will be over. Murat, I've come here to start a new job and it's only natural that I meet my fellow teachers and get involved in any social activities. Do you want that I just stay sitting in my room?"

I was getting mad again. I just couldn't understand his attitude.

"Call me when you get home please," he responded. "Enjoy your evening."

I could hear the dissatisfaction in his voice. I didn't like this behaviour and having to check in with him about everything I did.

"Thank you, bye."

The evening's dinner was a most enjoyable event; about twenty of us all sitting around a large table laden with the most delicious looking array of dishes I'd ever seen. A small Turkish quartet played soft music in the background and the restaurants décor was warm and exotic. Chatting to those either side of me and across from me, I soon felt like one of the family.

I met Paul, the Australian teacher who was actually Turkish and spoke the language perfectly. He was born in Australia to Turkish parents and had returned to Turkey to learn about his culture and find a Turkish wife. He seemed a sweet guy and I would be sharing some of my classes with him apparently.

Then there was the Canadian teacher, young and newly graduated and recently married to a beautiful young Ukrainian girl. Another Canadian also with a Ukrainian girl friend had been teaching in Izmit for a few years now.

There was an American husband and wife team, both teachers and probably closer in age to me. I think Angie was probably the oldest of the teachers, followed closely by me, but it didn't seem that age was any sort of issue here. We all just enjoyed this evening and shared our stories, our lives and our reasons for being in Turkey.

A few times through the evening my phone buzzed and I deliberately ignored it. I knew it was Murat. Who else could it be? He was the only one who had my number. I just wanted to enjoy this evening with my new colleagues and I didn't need his interrogations and commands. I knew that by not answering him, he would be getting more and more angrier with me but that was his problem. He didn't own me. I wasn't a child and I certainly wasn't his possession that he could order about.

Meeting all the teachers now, I was certain that I wanted to spend my first New Year's Eve in Turkey with this crowd. It would be fun. We planned on going dancing to a local night club and since I hadn't been in a night club since I don't know when, I wasn't going to let this opportunity fly by. My New Year was going to be off to a brilliant start and the decision to come and teach English in Turkey was definitely a positive move. I was happy.

Chapter Twenty Five

"Zoe, I won't allow it," he boomed over the phone. "My sister is expecting you and has prepared special food in your honour."

"You won't allow it? You won't allow me to go out?" I repeated. "I told you before that I wanted to celebrate with my new colleagues. It's important that I make these social connections," I replied.

I was aware that my voice was trembling slightly.

I was trying to stay calm and in control. I could feel his anger through the phone line. In my mind's eye, I could imagine his face, red and contorted. I had witnessed it before when he talked about Asli. All the wrinkles on his forehead and between his eyes seemed deeper and his eyes became squinted. His blood pressure was definitely hitting the higher levels of what is considered healthy.

"Zoe, I am demanding that you stay at Nihal's home this weekend. It is for your own safety. New Year's Eve can be dangerous," he continued.

"For God's sake, Murat, how is it dangerous? I'm going out with my fellow teachers to a night club and that's the end of it. I will go home when everyone else goes home. Angie and I will be together. I will have a few drinks and a few dances. That's it. Ok," I replied. "I will visit Nihal next weekend. Plus, if you are really concerned you can join us in Izmit."

"You know I have to work that night," he bellowed.

"Well, Murat, I'm sorry but sitting at home alone with your sister who I can't even communicate with, doesn't sound so inviting. So, I'll see you all next weekend or if you want to visit me here, you are always welcome."

It seemed to me that since I had moved to Turkey, he thought he owned me. It was the first cracks in our relationship and he was displaying all the traits of a chauvinistic domineering Turkish man. He would have to change this attitude because otherwise we would be over.

Angie and I hit the nightclub sometime around eleven. Outside was freezing and delicate snowflakes landed on our jackets and kissed our faces. Inside was hot and smoky. We soon found the rest of the teachers huddled together in a far corner. The music was pumping. A Turkish rock band was playing on the large stage and the dance floor was filled to capacity. Angie and I made our way to the bar to get a drink but it was a struggle. The crowd was thick and throbbing.

There were various floors to this establishment. We had checked them all out by navigating the narrow dimly lit stairwell. The top floor was less packed and had rock music playing in the background. Here at least you could have a bit of a chat. Down on the second floor the band was so loud that there was no chance of any sort of conversation. We could only dance and dance is what we did. We danced the night away in this dark smoke filled pit. It felt like a pit, or a dungeon. I looked around. There was no windows, no exit signs. Surely, if a fire was to break out we would all be doomed as everyone rushed for the small narrow stairway to the street. I remember thinking that an establishment like this would never be allowed to operate in Australia. I could see how it could be a death trap. But this is Turkey and everything and anything goes. Even the recent 'no smoking inside' laws were not always heeded. I noticed that this law didn't apply on rainy or extremely cold days and it certainly didn't apply here tonight in the nightclub.

The countdown to midnight was soon approaching and we fought our way through to the bar to refill our glasses in readiness to greet the New Year. I checked my phone. Seven missed calls. There was no possible way I could have heard them or been able to talk.

The music stopped and the countdown had begun. The crowd chanting in Turkish......... *üç, iki, bir......Mutlu Yillar*.......Happy New Year! As a group of English teachers, coming together in a foreign country, away from our families and loved ones, we all kissed and hugged each other. We were now family. We were the closest thing we had to familiar and we bonded in this moment. The music roared and we danced on through the night.

I had to drag myself away to go outside and call Murat. Nine missed calls now. He wasn't going to be happy.

"Happy New Year, Murat," I screamed into the phone trying to sound jovial.

"Where are you?" he replied.

"We're still at the night club. It's been a really fun night. We'll be heading home shortly."

I tried to console him before he started up again with the usual rant.

"One of the teachers, Jeff from England, is going to drive me and Angie home. So you don't need to worry," I continued.

"And who is this Jeff? Can you really trust him?" Murat asked.

"Of course, he's one of the teachers here. Anyway, how was your evening?"

"The usual," replied Murat. "Nothing special. I tried to call you many times."

"Yes, I saw. The music was so loud I didn't hear it. Sorry. Anyway, I had better get back inside. It's freezing out here. Talk to you tomorrow, Ok?"

I ended our call with kisses but I knew he was angry with me. I knew I'd be in for a good lecture tomorrow. This wasn't going to work. I was an Australian woman and he was a Turkish man. It was becoming apparent to me now that the cultural differences were actually greater than we had at first envisaged.

My first New Year's Eve in Turkey had been a memorable one and I hadn't danced like that since my twenties. It felt liberating and rejuvenating. I knew I was going to enjoy my time living and teaching here. It was all so exciting and exotic. As much as I had realised my new found love for Turkey, similarly I realised that my relationship with Murat was probably doomed. I knew he wouldn't, couldn't, change his ways and I was not prepared to be controlled and dominated. It seemed to me that this fairy tale romance would soon run its course.

Chapter Twenty Six

"Good morning, students. My name is Zoe. I am from Australia, and I am your teacher for this course of English."

My stomach was a mess but I had to get through this first lesson. All eyes were eagerly upon me. The classroom was very modern and set up with the student's chairs in a large semicircle formation. The chairs had small fold up desks attached. The back of the classroom was all windows looking down towards the expressway, rail tracks and the sea. In the front of the classroom, where I stood, was a large whiteboard and above that a picture of Turkey's national hero and great leader, Mustafa Kemal Atatürk.

A lovely little mosque was situated not far from the school. This mosque was built by *Mimar Sinan,* the famous Ottoman architect who is accredited with the construction of the magnificent *Selimiye Mosque* in Edirne and the *Suleiman Mosque* in Istanbul. He trained many students in his day, one of whom was responsible for the construction of Istanbul's stunning *Sultan Ahmed* or *Blue Mosque* as it's more commonly known. When the *ezan* echoed from the minarets of our neighbouring mosque, my class would come to a complete stop and we would all wait in silence for its passing.

Izmit was a very conservative town and half of my students were covered girls. That was, they voluntarily wore the head scarf. It wasn't compulsory and in fact at this time, it was actually forbidden to wear the headscarf to university or in any government offices. Still these girls chose to wear it when they could. I even heard that they would wear wigs to university to cover their heads since the head scarf was banned. These very girls that covered their heads paradoxically had no problem wearing a face load of makeup and very tight jeans. I had a lot to learn about my new country and its customs and religion and what was acceptable and what wasn't. Another example was that for the devout, alcohol was forbidden and yet smoking was all the rage and it seemed every one of my students smoked. I decided I would need to tread lightly and try to absorb as much of the history, culture and customs, as I could and not question too much.

My first lesson went smoothly as the students really were the most sweetest and respectful group of young people. They were happy to hear about my life in Australia and I was open to all their questions, even the very personal ones.

"How old are you, teacher?"

"Where is your husband?"

"Do you have children?"

I found this line of questioning slightly intrusive but answered as best and as honest as I could. I preferred the questions about Australia and tried my best to steer the class that way.

"Does anyone know the capital city of Australia?" I asked.

"No, it isn't Sydney or Melbourne. Anyone heard of Canberra? No?"

"Yes, I have seen many kangaroos."

"Yes, we do have a lot of spiders and snakes."

"Yes, sharks are a big problem."

Before I knew it the buzzer sounded, signalling a very welcomed ten minute tea break up on the terrace. It seemed that my first lesson had gone well and I realised that educating these students about Australia was a good starting point.

As I got my coffee and headed out onto the terrace for some fresh air, I realised I had a small following of students. Of course most of them came out to smoke and also to get some relief from the stifling heat inside the classroom. The heating in our school more than compensated for the low temperatures outside and I needed to remember to wear something lighter to class tomorrow.

"My teacher, Izmit good city?"

"It is a lovely city," I replied.

"My teacher, you like?" asked Emre, as he offered me a cigarette.

"No thank you, Emre," I replied.

"My teacher, take photo?" asked one of the girls.

It was going to take a day or two to learn all their names.

"Sure. Is it Fatma?" I replied as we huddled together for a selfie.

I was starting to relax now as I realised that these beautiful young people didn't bite. They were extremely welcoming and kind and I felt honoured to have the task of teaching them English.

Class resumed and we continued on with our discussion about Australia and then they were more than happy to tell me about their country.

"Have you eaten *manti*, my teacher?"

Manti I learnt was a sort of Turkish dumpling served with yoghurt and a spicy tomato sauce on top. It was obviously a class favourite as my students insisted that they would take me to the best *manti* place in town.

They continued to rattle off the names of other Turkish dishes that I needed to try; *lahmucan* a thin pizza style dish, *pide* another pizza style dish, *hamsi* grilled anchovies. I began to write these things down and soon realised that whilst I was going to teach them English they were going to teach me so much about their country too.

That first day turned out to be a real delight and I felt that I had established a real rapport with my students. By learning all of their names and showing a genuine interest in their lives and culture, we bonded well and I made many new friendships. Within no time at all, my students were taking me to their favourite restaurants and teaching me about their delicious cuisine. I was invited to meet their parents and I even receive gifts.

One day a student brought me in a lunchbox full of *dolma* or vine leaves stuffed with savoury rice, which she had made with her mother and grandmother. I soon realised that I loved *dolma*. This Turkish speciality got its name from the minibuses called *dolmuş*. These types of small buses serviced the smaller towns and villages and were usually stuffed to capacity hence the name meaning stuffed.

Another day a student brought in a box of the honey and pistachio pastries called *baklava,* which we all shared at break time. I was having such a rewarding and life changing experience and I was so grateful for these moments enjoyed with my students. Turkey was so different from what I was used to in Australia and I was enjoying every minute, soaking in its uniqueness and rich culture.

I had visited Nihal the next weekend, taking the one hour bus into Istanbul and then the underground rail system out to the suburb of Bakırköy. It was quite an excursion for me but I followed Murat's instructions and eventually found my way. I found people most obliging and happy to help me with directions despite my lack of Turkish and their lack of English.

Nihal was very welcoming. As she opened the door, her face lit up with happiness and she grabbed me and kissed me on both cheeks. She pulled me in and after removing my shoes, she offered me some of her brightly coloured and sequined slippers. I was happy to walk around in my socks but she insisted I wear a pair of her slippers. She was fussing over me and it did feel nice. Again we didn't share a language but it seemed to work. Eventually, we sat down to a massive feast that she had prepared. Murat would be home soon and I would spend the night with them returning to Izmit the next day for school again on Monday.

Nihal and I tried to communicate using charades and we laughed so much but it was draining. I was grateful when her daughter Meryem finally arrived home and could translate for us.

"How do you like living in Izmit?" she asked.

"So far, it's been wonderful. I'm sorry I didn't make it here last weekend but I had already made plans with my colleagues and you know I want to fit in and make friends there."

"We understand, of course. It's important that you make some friends," replied Meryem.

How come she could understand and yet Murat was still angry with me, I thought to myself? What was he thinking? He would be arriving home from work soon and I was excited to see him but also a little anxious. I was expecting a telling off. It had been at least a couple of weeks now since we had last been together. We had talked everyday on the phone and I had kept him informed about my classes and my students. I was still living out at the Yuvacik staff housing with Angie and he seemed to be a little more at ease with that now. In fact, the next weekend he had holidays and was going to come and stay with me, so he said.

I heard his key in the door and felt goose bumps. Meryem was smiling at me.

"You are happy?" she said.

Murat burst into the room and came straight towards me, holding me tight in his arms and kissing me on the cheek. He felt like home. I breathed in the warmth of his embrace and looked forward to our night together. There would be little romance with his sister and niece sleeping in the next room, but just to be held would be enough.

"How are you, my darling?" he asked as removed his jacket and joined us at the table. Nihal poured him tea and organised his plate with a selection of foods from her banquet. To my relief, he didn't even bring up New Year's Eve or my decision to disobey him. Thankfully I thought as I could see that it would have developed into an argument. He was wise to not press that any further.

The weekend had been a relaxing and peaceful time reconnecting with Murat and easing any concerns he had about my time in Izmit. I looked forward to his visit the next weekend and was already planning where we would explore. As it soon became time for me to travel home, Murat drove me to the bus station and with a bag load of food and goodies from Nihal, I boarded the Metro bus bound for Izmit, followed by the small local bus back to my new home in Yuvacik.

Chapter Twenty Seven

Classes were becoming easier and I was no longer anxious about my lessons. I was actually enjoying them. Lesson preparation was stress-free as we had text books to follow and all I needed to do was to prepare some interesting exercises to compliment the texts. Admittedly, the students found the text books boring and that's why it was necessary to have other fun activities and games prepared.

The text books covered all the necessary skills of reading, writing, listening and speaking and of course, the dread of every English teacher, grammar. What I soon realised was that my students' knowledge of grammar was probably on par if not better than mine. They had been drilled in the grammar. Their real problems were speaking and that's where I felt I excelled the most. Firstly, I was a very good talker for sure with lots of stories and experiences to share. Secondly, I could easily get my students to talk and encourage them not to be shy or self-conscious. After all, as I explained to them, they are more skilled than me as I only spoke English whilst they spoke two languages.

Fortunately for me, most of my classes were at intermediate or advanced level which meant that communication wasn't a problem and we could have some very interesting discussions and debates. The topic my students were most knowledgeable about and loved to talk about was there great leader Mustafa Kemal Atatürk. I didn't dare tell them that before coming to Turkey, I had never ever heard of him.

During my time in Izmit I learnt a lot about him and his heroism during the First World War and his founding of the Republic of Turkey in 1923. He really was a revolutionary in every way; he introduced European style dress codes, doing away with the *fez* and head scarf, he brought in the Gregorian calendar instead of the Islamic one, he made Sunday a day of rest as in Europe and he introduced the Roman alphabet instead of the Arabic letters which were previously used. The more I read and learnt about him, I was really impressed and a bit ashamed that I had never heard of him before.

One thing I did notice with my students, however, was their total lack of knowledge of anything beyond Turkey. Sometimes I was blown away when, for example, none of them had heard of the Beatles. I mean I thought the whole world knew of the Beatles. Another example was when I asked my class, who knew of William Shakespeare and one student told me that he was a famous artist. This set me on a course to try to expand their world and knowledge of countries beyond their borders. A majority of my students couldn't even name the countries that bordered Turkey and to ask them the capital cities of other countries was also a huge disappointment. I soon realised my task was much bigger than just teaching them English.

One sweet guy in one of my classes was called Süleyman. He was a rather large and gentle giant, sweet and shy. I was shocked to witness how many times other students called him 'fat'. Even he would agree and say "Yes, I'm very fat." Coming from Australia, where we are always so politically correct and would never comment on someone's size, this always astonished me. They seemed to have no inhibitions or stigmas attached to these traits. It was what it was.

From the very first lesson, I had been exposed to their intrusive questioning which again, coming from Australia, we just would never ask. These sorts of questions about our age and personal life were something that we would only share with our closest friends. That wasn't the case in Turkey. Here my students constantly asked about my age, if I was rich, if I was married and how many children did I have.

"My teacher, do you like Turkey?" asked Serpil.

This was a question that I was asked frequently by my students. There was no denying that the Turkish people that I met were fiercely patriotic and loved their country above all else but they also needed to hear me say it.

"Well, I've only been here for a short time as you know, but so far I am very happy here. Your country has been very welcoming and friendly to me," I replied.

"My teacher, why did you leave Australia? Don't you like it?" asked Mustafa.

"Of course, I love Australia but I wanted an adventure. I wanted to experience living in another country," I replied.

They clearly couldn't fathom that idea.

"Which country do you love best, Australia or Turkey?" asked Ismail.

"I love them both. Australia is my country and so of course I love it very much. Turkey is my adoptive country and I love it here too," I replied as diplomatically as I could.

Questioning about my marriage, lead me to explain that I was getting a divorce. This resulted in my receiving much sympathy and sad faces. I think they saw me as a sad tragic case. It was even suggested to me that if I returned to my husband and apologised for my wrong doings, he might take me back. It was just assumed that I was the wrong doer. They couldn't fathom the idea that I was happy and enjoyed living alone, and I didn't want to go back. They couldn't comprehend that a woman could be quite satisfied with her life without a husband. Of course, they didn't know about Murat. But things with Murat were about to take a massive dive.

I was looking forward to his visit this coming weekend. We had talked every evening and Murat had booked us a room in a five star hotel overlooking the sea. It wasn't too far away, he said and a much better option than staying at the staff housing with Angie. Also the thought of my single mattress on the floor didn't quite appeal to Murat's sense of adventure. We planned on touring a little around the area and maybe even going up to the ski fields for a look. We would enjoy a romantic dinner in the hotel restaurant, a lazy morning in bed followed by a late breakfast before heading home. It sounded perfect.

Chapter Twenty Eight

Come Friday evening, I was beginning to get a little concerned as he hadn't rang me yet and it was past the time of his usual evening call. I knew that he had finished work already. Perhaps he was busy, caught in traffic, any number of things could be the reason, but I was beginning to have my suspicions. I had a fluttery feeling in the pit of my stomach. Was it my intuition kicking in? Not this weekend, please God. I was so looking forward to getting away, just the two of us.

I went to bed that night with a heavy heart and I had constantly checked my phone to see if I had missed a call or a message. Was the volume up? Was the battery charged? I knew something bad had happened. I knew it was probably something to do with his wife. There was nothing I could do. I didn't dare call him. We had agreed that I would only call him when I knew he was at work but otherwise it was best if he called me. If he wasn't at work, I had no way of knowing if he was with his sons, or her, or some other family member. It did make me feel like 'the other woman' but I knew the way it was and I certainly never wanted to inflame the situation. So, tossing and turning, I waited patiently for his call.

No call from Murat. I sat with Angela quietly drinking my coffee and eating the mandarins I had bought for breakfast. I was thinking to myself what could have happened? Of course, I was imagining the worst. Obviously something wasn't right. I had gone through so many scenarios in my head throughout the night. It had been a long sleepless night and I was exhausted.

"Aren't you going away this weekend?" asked Angie.

"Not sure," I replied.

It was the first time that I had opened up to Angie and told her the entire story.

"I suspect that his wife has found out that I am in the country and all hell has broke loose," I added.

Well, I had resigned myself to the fact that he wasn't coming. I was feeling down and upset and also wanted to know what had happened. I stood at my window gazing out at the white blanket of snow that covered the roofs of the neighbouring cottages and their gardens. In front of our block of flats someone had swept the snow from the footpath and a small pile of snow and leaves sat to the side. A couple of young boys were out kicking about and enjoying the winter wonderland. I watched their games and for the moment, my thoughts were lost in the snow.

Suddenly, my phone buzzed and vibrated on the table. I now had a few of the teachers' phone numbers in my phone so it could have been anyone. I picked it up and to my relief, saw that it was Murat.

"Hello," I answered excitedly.

There was nothing but silence.

"Hello. Murat?" I answered again.

Just silence. A long drawn out silence and then it hung up.

Hmm…..this wasn't good, I thought to myself. Things were definitely strange and even though I was holding on to hope, I was beginning to realise that this weekend wasn't going to happen. Somehow, she must have found out that I was in Turkey. Oh poor Murat; I could only wait and be patient. Hopefully things weren't as bad as I was envisaging right now.

She had always threatened that his sons would disown him and that she would make him pay dearly in the courts if he continued his relationship with me. She and her family would ruin him and his reputation, she had claimed. She even hit him. She was one very angry and

196

scary Turkish woman and as I had already experienced her anger on my Australian phone, I certainly didn't look forward to anymore of her aggressive behaviour.

It was she that had wanted the divorce. It was she that had thrown him out of the family home. So why now is she so bothered about who he sees? How did she get my new number? How did Murat let that happen? Was this all worth it? Maybe Murat and I needed to take a break. He needed to get his life sorted. I really didn't want any part of this drama. My mind was awash with all these thoughts. There was a small storm brewing in my gut and I was beginning to experience a piercing ache in my temples.

My phone buzzed and vibrated again. I was scared to answer it this time. I knew that it wasn't going to be good.

"Hello, Murat," I answered meekly.

This time my voice was soft and slightly shaky.

A barrage of angry screaming Turkish accosted my ears. It was all gibberish to me, but I certainly got the message; her message. She was seething, almost murderous in her tirade of words. I could hear Murat in the background obviously trying to settle her and take back his phone. This was high drama like I had never experienced before. I didn't know whether to just hang up or to wait till she was done.

"Zoe," it was Murat now.

His voice was strained.

"Zoe, I'm sorry but she knows that you are in Turkey. She's going mad. I'm so sorry," he cried.

He tried to explain what had happened. All the time, I could hear her in the background screaming and it sounded like she was throwing things around.

"Yesterday after I finished my work, I went to my house to see the boys and to pick up some extra winter clothes. I wanted my big snow jacket," he explained. "When I got home, I realised that I had left my phone there or she had taken it from my bag."

I couldn't believe that he had been as reckless and clumsy as to leave his phone unattended and therefore giving her the opportunity to take it.

"How, Murat? How could you do that?" I pleaded.

Heat was rising in my cheeks and I could feel tears welling in my eyes.

"I'm sorry, darling. I just didn't think. She must have taken it when I was talking with the boys. My bag was on the kitchen table."

"Murat, you've spoiled everything now," I cried.

"This morning I returned to the house to collect my phone and she was waiting for me," he continued. "She's been going wild. She's been screaming and hitting me. She has poisoned the boys against me. Really I don't know what to do?"

"Murat, I think in all reality we have to end our relationship now. You need to sort out your life," I cried. "I don't want the responsibility of your sons and family disowning you. This is just too much for me to handle."

"I'm sorry, darling." I could hear the tremble in his voice.

"I'm sorry too, Murat," I replied.

And I was sorry. It was unfair and unjust. She didn't want him but she didn't want anyone else to have him either. He needed to sort this out on his own without me in the picture. Also, I was in a foreign country and not totally aware of how things went down. What if she sent someone after me? What if she wanted to cause me harm? I needed to back right out of this relationship now and stay as far away as possible.

"I'm sorry Murat, but I don't want this anymore," I cried.

"But I love you Zoe. I don't know what to do. I hate her," he said.

"I know, but it's just not working out. Let's leave it for a while and see how you go with organising your divorce and getting your sons back. Good bye Murat."

I was trying to be the strong one. I could see the situation more clearly and I needed to make the decision or at least give Murat a way out. I wasn't even sure if I wanted to spend my life with him. I did love him now, but his controlling ways had scared me. It was best to take a good long break and see what happens in the future.

For the meantime, I would throw myself into my new career. I had a great group of new friends at school and Matt would be here in a month's time. I had that to focus on. It was going to be awesome. I needed to spend my time now finding a new flat in town for the two of us.

I decided that a flat in the centre of town would be the best as I could walk to work and all the shops were at my convenience. Yuvacik was just too far away and those late night buses home in the freezing temperatures were becoming a real chore now. Yes, I had plenty to keep me busy and Murat had plenty he needed to work out too.

"Ok, Angie, what do you feel like doing today?" I called out to my house mate.

The idea of finding a decent flat in a foreign country where I have no knowledge of the language did seem a daunting task. I was at first overwhelmed by the enormity of this mission. I didn't even know where to start. I still had the occasional call from Murat but I didn't want to ask for his help and add to his already stressful life. He had his own problems to deal with.

"So how do I go about finding a furnished flat in Izmit?" I asked Karen at school one day.

"Well, there are agencies that can help you but they will charge you a lot of money and are notorious for cheating foreigners. You will see the sign *Emlak*, but I don't recommend them," she replied.

"The best idea is to walk around the area that you like and look for a sign in the window that says *kiralik* which means 'for rent'," she continued. "I don't know your chances of finding a furnished flat but you can try. Also put the message out with your students. Often their families may have a flat for rent."

This all sounded like good advice and as well as announcing to my students that I was looking for a small furnished flat in town, I began scouring the immediate area for *kiralik* signs.

Out of town in the newer suburbs it was much easier to find a modern and furnished flat but I didn't want to have to travel by bus. Also I reasoned that with Matt living here too, I wanted it to be easy to see him between classes and for him to join me at school. I focused my search on an area within a maximum ten minute walk to work. The buildings in this area were admittedly over thirty years old but the fact that they had withstood the earthquake of 1999, meant that they were strong and hopefully safe for living.

It was through the help of a student that I eventually found the flat that was to be our home for the most part of the year. It was up on the fourth floor of a six floor building that had been built in the sixties. It had suffered only minor damage during the earthquake and its location was perfect, about a three minute walk to school.

It had a small elevator that rattled slowly up to the fourth floor and as we entered the flat, I was amused by the brightly painted walls. One bedroom was bright pink whilst the other was bright blue. The paint job had been done recently and paint splatters covered the also newly laid timber laminate flooring. What a shame they hadn't thought about a drop sheet I thought.

It overlooked the central square and was basically next to the city council building. It had lots of windows with views out to the distant mountains and down on to the bustling streets below. The window in the kitchen looked down at a huge neon sign announcing the time and temperature. Now that could be handy, I thought. The kitchen was old but the cupboards looked to be in a reasonable condition. Just the linoleum on the kitchen floor was cracked and dirty. It would need a good scrub with bleach. The bathroom was large and adequate. This flat wasn't furnished. The kitchen had no appliances and I would have to buy a small hotplate at the very least. However, as the location was perfect, I decided to take it. On Karen's advice I hired a cleaning lady to come in for a day and give it a thorough scrubbing.

I signed a six month lease and didn't realise at the time that I was paying way too much, but what the heck I had a new flat. Now I needed to get it ready for Matt's arrival. I would just buy the most necessary items to get us by for the next six months or so.

Another student came with me and helped me buy two single mattresses. A mattress on the floor had been comfortable enough at Yuvacik and so I thought we could manage that way at our new flat too. I needed to buy some extra linen for Matt. I bought two small tables: one for the kitchen and one for my laptop and office area. I bought two chairs, a couple of pots and pans, a hotplate, toaster, cutlery and enough crockery for two. The flat had an efficient gas heating system and as for refrigeration, I could just put any food stuffs out on the window ledge or balcony where night temperatures at this time of year were usually below zero.

For Wi-Fi, I approached my neighbour and asked for her password in exchange for my paying half of her monthly contract fee. She was most happy as was I, as I didn't want to commit to a two year contract. I was really lucky in that many of my students helped me with translations and getting all the necessary tasks done.

I needed to change the gas, water and electricity accounts into my name and pay the deposits to open the accounts. Because I didn't have residency, I couldn't put these accounts in my name. My school helped me there and two of the young office girls were able to open the electricity and water accounts for me in their names. For the gas account a student was suggested and he also happily opened the account in his name. This meant that all deposits that I paid were in these other peoples' names and I had to trust that when I wanted to close the accounts that I would receive the deposits back. We live and learn.

My moving into my new home when smoothly as I only had a suitcase to bring over and some bed linen and pillows. Angie was disappointed that I was leaving but she had made no effort to find herself a flat. Her main preoccupation was still finding a church and the religion stuff was getting to be a drag. She had other peculiarities that I was tiring of too. She would eat whatever food I had bought and put in the fridge. This meant that when I went to have my breakfast or a snack, some cheese and olives for example, there was nothing left. I couldn't believe it. We weren't college students, after all. She would drink my coffee and milk and never replace anything. She even used my protein powder which wasn't cheap and was my morning drink before classes. In the end, I had to hide these things in my suitcase and just hoped she didn't go in there too.

One night I was awoken from my sleep with her banging on my bedroom door and calling out my name. Thinking that there was some sort of an emergency, I jumped out of bed and opened my door.

"What's wrong?" I asked.

"I just wanted to tell you that I am going to call home to the States on skype and it might wake you," she replied.

I couldn't see the logic in this as she had clearly just woken me to tell me this astounding news. Other nights she walked around the flat at all hours and had all the lights on. I needed to cover up the small window in my bedroom door to block out the light as it kept me awake.

Another day I had come home from work to find the flat cold and dark and Angie sitting on the floor in the corner.

"Why are you sitting in the cold and dark?" I asked.

The usually warm flat was freezing.

"There's no electricity," she replied.

The lights had been on in the entrance and the elevator had worked fine. I tried our light switch.

"Did you try the fuse box?" I asked.

"No. What's that?" she replied.

I couldn't believe that she could be so helpless. By the light of my phone I located the fuse box just inside the main door and flicked the switch.

"Let there be light," I exclaimed triumphantly.

It was becoming obvious to me that she had a few psychological issues and I was thankful that I was moving out. We had shared some enjoyable times but I was always aware that she just seemed out of touch and definitely out of her depth here in Turkey. Living abroad isn't for everyone. You need to have the desire and the ability to assimilate into your new culture, and for Angie this just wasn't working.

After I left the apartment in Yuvacik, Angie's fate seemed to spiral out of control. I began to hear crazy tales from the other teachers about her constant quest to find churches and the students didn't like her at all. She definitely had issues. It was just a matter of time before she was asked to leave the school and she immediately flew back to Washington where I'm sure she would have been much happier.

I was reasonable satisfied in my new flat. Admittedly, it was sparsely furnished or as I liked to call it, the minimalist look, but it did have a massively deep bath tub.

Coming home from work on those freezing cold nights, nothing was more satisfying than a long soak in my bubble filled tub. It was my perfect indulgence. It was my time to just chill, relax, meditate and feel blessed for my new life. I had all the basics and most importantly, this flat was so warm. The heating system worked brilliantly and even if it was snowing outside, inside I was as snug as a bug in a rug.

Most days I ate out as food in Turkey was so cheap, but I could make a toast and cook an egg for breakfast and I had bought a French press for my morning coffee. I was quite comfortable by now and hoped Matt would feel so too.

My flat was surrounded by a good assortment of restaurants and cafes. There was also a fine selection of shops on my street. Just across the road I had my cheese shop. A whole shop dedicated to cheese. It took a couple of weeks for the staff there to realise that I was actually living in Izmit and a regular customer. They were very friendly and went out of their way to help me and always offered me tastings of the different cheeses. I was in cheese heaven. They also had huge vats of olives and again I would sample and take home my selection.

Directly downstairs and next to the entrance of my building was a washing machine and flower shop. I was often amused by the funny combination of products being sold in the one store but I did like to regularly buy a bunch of fresh flowers to brighten up the kitchen. Next to this store was a Chinese thrift store where you could buy everything for really cheap. That's where I got my fold-up tables and chairs and all the crockery and cutlery for the kitchen. I also bought a clothes stand for my jacket and scarves as I had no wardrobes. My towels, sheets and bath mat all came from there too, as well as candles and incense from India.

There was a supermarket was just around the corner and there I could buy all the groceries I needed. What was noticeable was the lack of variety. In Australia there would be a whole aisle dedicated to crackers and biscuits but here in Turkey there was usually just the one choice. The fruit and vegetables were so fresh and full of flavour. My diet consisted mostly of mandarins and oranges and of course, the irresistible cheeses and olives. I didn't miss any particular foods from Australia as I was so excited to try all the new foods on offer.

I did however, dislike offal and that was something I wouldn't ever eat, despite my students' encouragement to do so. A favourite dish was *Kokoreç* which was lamb and goats intestines grilled on a rotisserie. There were so many *Kokoreç* shops around that I gathered it must be a very popular dish but I just couldn't bring myself to try it. The thought of it turned my stomach as did *işkembe çorbası* or tripe soup. My students swore by this soup as the perfect hangover cure but luckily I never had a hangover and nothing would ever make me eat that either. There were soup salons that only opened after midnight and served only *işkembe çorbası* so I guess its claim to fame for as a hangover cure was true.

In the mornings I would awaken to the call of a street vendor downstairs below my windows selling his produce. I could look out and see what was on offer. Usually it was strawberries or nuts or *simit*. It was a whole new world to me. My neighbours would lower down a bucket on a rope from their window and the vendor would simple put their stack of breakfast *simit* into the bucket and then they would haul it back up; such ingenuity.

A couple of streets away there was a DVD shop that Sue had shown me. Whenever she was in Izmit she went there for her movie fix. This shop sold pirated copies of all the Hollywood blockbusters, sometimes even before they were officially released. Of course, we realised that this business was highly illegal and in any other country would be swiftly closed down, but this was Turkey. We would browse through the huge selection of movies and series and buy our evening entertainment for about fifty cents a pop. I got to buy the whole collection of seasons of Desperate Housewives that I had wanted to see for years.

It just seemed to me that no matter what you wanted or needed, you could find it here in the streets of Izmit and you could find it cheap. That's as long as you weren't cheated or tricked which was something I learnt to be constantly aware of.

Chapter Twenty Nine

Sadly, my chats with Murat were a lot less frequent now. I often wondered how he was doing. The last time he had called, he had told me that he had no options left to him but to move back into the family home. He had tried to assure me that he was sleeping in the spare room, but I wasn't concerned about that. I knew that we would never have worked out long term anyway, so it was all for the best.

He had come into my life at a time when I had needed him. I had needed something and he was the impetus for my realisation that there was a lot of living still left for me to do. Looking back I didn't regret one single day and today I could say I was truly happy. I was doing a very rewarding job and I had made lots of new friendships and to top it all off, Matt would be arriving soon.

Sue, my mentor from Adapazari had become a very close friend in a short space of time. I guess when you are living in a foreign country you seek out the friendships of like-minded people and if you are lucky they are people you genuinely like. I have to say that just because we come from similar cultures it doesn't always mean that we will be friends. There were a couple of the teachers at school that I just knew I could never be friends with. From their behaviour, the way they adapted to their new country, their criticisms of their Turkish students and Turkey in general, I just knew that we had nothing in common and probably would never be friends.

With Sue it was entirely different. We had clicked from our very first skype call back in Australia. She was great fun. We had met for our first lunch date in Izmit. After all the skype chats we were finally meeting in person. I couldn't help pinching myself when I realised that after all those weeks chatting with Sue over skype, now I was here. I was in Turkey and I was teaching English. That first meeting with Sue really cemented our friendship.

The next time we got together, I had visited her in Adapazari. She drove a beat up jeep and it was so much fun as she whizzed around town showing me the sights. We drove out to Lake Sapanca, a tranquil fresh water lake on the outskirts of town. Lake Sapanca had picnic areas and peaceful walking trails, as well as a well-known and very expensive spa that was frequented by many Turkish celebrities. There was also a restaurant where we decided to stop for our lunch and relax a little after the stress of Sue's driving.

"You have to drive aggressively here," she said as I was holding on tight to my seat.

"If they sense any weakness in you, they'll cut in and run you off the road," she continued.

I could see that she knew what she was talking about. Turkish drivers didn't seem to pay any attention to road signs or even the lights and they loved to honk their horns. In my mind, Sue was very brave to wander out onto the roads. It wasn't something I thought I could do.

Sue had moved to Adapazari with her husband who was the managing director of a well-known international company located there. They had a big house, company cars, a cleaner, a gardener, a swimming pool and the whole works. They had enjoyed an extremely comfortable and luxurious life. Sadly, one day at work, her husband had suffered a massive heart attack and died. It was sudden and a shock to everyone as he was only in his mid-fifties.

After the sorrow had become slightly more bearable, Sue was left with nothing, the house and cars were gone. It was either move back to England or she could endeavour to make a life for herself in Turkey. She chose the latter and secured a teaching job at one of the academies where she had previously volunteered. They were kind enough to offer her a fulltime teaching job and a small furnished studio apartment. Sue had enjoyed her life in Turkey and she and her husband had had some wonderful experiences and lots of amazing memories and she wasn't ready just yet to walk away from that.

I, of course, told Sue my entire tale of woe, from the arrival of Murat's letter in my letter box to our romantic getaway in Cappadocia to my now teaching English in Izmit. I told her of the latest developments with his wife and his decision to move back home with her.

"Just forget about him," she advised. "It's not worth the heart ache and I can tell you, he will never leave his wife."

I was quite sure that she was right. I really enjoyed my time spent with Sue. We could talk so much about anything and everything. One day we had decided to go and spend the day in Istanbul. Sue knew Istanbul very well and was going to show me around some of her favourite places. We would both take our individual buses, hers from Adapazari and mine from Izmit and we would meet at the Harem bus station or *otogar*. From there we would take the ferry boat to Eminönü where we could begin our day's exploration.

The ferry boat was comfortably warm and we bought *çay* from the canteen and enjoying the ride, we happily chatted on about our work and lives. We were totally oblivious to the fact that we had arrived. Hundreds of passengers had already disembarked and we were the only passengers left aboard. We were still chatting away when to our shock and surprise an attendant had come to tell us that we were now in Eminönü and needed to disembark.

Another day, after exploring the exciting area of Taksim and Istiklal Avenue, we had stumbled onto the enchanting French Street, known originally as *Cezayir* or *Fransiz Sok*. After being enticed by a gorgeous young Turkish waiter, we had decided to take a seat and have some dinner. Of course, we ordered a bottle of wine too. We deserved it. It had been a magical day and we were already weary from all our walking and talking. Our meal was superb and the location was exotic. The entire lane had beautifully restored buildings painted a rose pink colour and was lit up with fairy lights hanging between the bars and restaurants. We were relaxed on comfortable chairs with colourful cushions, enjoying the moment and reflecting on our lives in Turkey.

"Christ, its nine thirty five. The last ferry back to Harem is at ten. We need to move it," screamed Sue.

We paid our bill and frantically made our way down the steep hill to the water front. The fresh air and the alcohol had taken its effect and we were stumbling, screaming and laughing as we tackled the cobble stones and arrived just in time to board the last ferry boat back to Harem. We laughed so much but the reality was that if we had missed that ferry crossing, we would have had to have got a hotel for the night. I could only imagine what Murat would have had to say about that, if he was still in my life. I was sort of grateful that he wasn't. I was definitely in love with Turkey and I could never have enjoyed it the same way with Murat controlling my every move.

Chapter Thirty

My teaching career was off to an impressive start. My confidence was growing with each and every lesson. Sometimes I would have morning classes from ten till two, but I preferred the evening classes from six till ten, especially since I no longer had to take the long bus trip back to Yuvacik. Yes, moving into town was a brilliant move and a definite boost to my social life.

Another new teacher to the school was Mandy from the United States. She was ex-army and quite loud and at times rather obnoxious. She was a drinker, a big drinker and it wasn't long before she had herself a fine reputation. Beer was her poison and there had been many occasions when she had to be carried home or at least put into a taxi. Her flat mates had had enough of her. She seemed to get on everyone's bad side. She constantly borrowed money that she never paid back. She helped herself to her flatmates beverages in the fridge, be it coke cola or beer. Whilst the teachers held her in disdain, most of the students loved her. She did have a cheeky and fun side to her personality and that came out in her classes, especially the ones she gave after a beer or two.

I had heard all the gossip and tried to keep clear of Mandy but one day after morning classes, she invited me out for a lunchtime drink down on the seafront. This was probably because she had exhausted all other friendships. Though I was wary, I felt that I couldn't really say no. I didn't have a fast enough excuse. Well it was day time, I reasoned. A couple hours down by the sea front would be nice. Surely nothing could go wrong. It actually started off well and I can remember thinking that she wasn't as bad as everyone had said. We had some interesting conversation.

The gossip had painted a rather bad picture of Mandy and her behaviour but so far she seemed to be acting quite normal. She told me some of her story; she had been married to a fellow soldier who had done a couple of tours to Iraq, she was now divorced, she had two children who now lived with their father as she had lost custody through the courts and for some reason, that she didn't disclose, she had also lost her army career. She had gone to Prague to do her TEFL course and was as newly qualified as me. I sensed a deep sadness in Mandy. I felt for her and couldn't see that she was as bad as everyone had said. Well, I was soon to learn the hard way.

We had crossed the overpass and on to the park land that ran along the waterfront. Strolling along through the well-kept gardens we eventually stopped at a little restaurant that had tables out on an open terrace that faced the sea. It was a beautiful sunny February day with brilliant blue skies but still quite chilly. We chose a table near one of the gas heaters and ordered two beers. Mandy drank that first pint down before I was even a quarter of the way through mine. I explained to her that I wasn't really a beer drinker and that a pint was really too much for me but before I knew it she had signalled the waiter and two more pints arrived.

"Ok, please don't order me anymore drinks," I said.

I was feeling slightly annoyed now as I looked at my beers lining up. Mandy was happily chugging down her second pint.

"Hey, look at those two guys over there," she said with a smile. "What are they drinking?"

I was familiar with this national drink of Turkey called *raki,* because it was Murat's drink of choice. It was aniseed flavoured and when you added water, it turned a cloudy white colour. It was delicious but I was well aware of its strength; forty to fifty percent alcohol. I explained all this to Mandy as she continued to eye these two innocent

Turkish guys, whose table was now covered with a healthy selection of appetizers known as *meze*.

With Mandy's constant staring and smiling, it wasn't long before we were invited to join their table and share in their banquet. They were both local business men and fortunately for us, one of them spoke very good English. We chatted happily about our jobs as English teachers and where we were from, the usual conversation one has with people that they just meet. Mandy had downed her second pint of beer and was on to mine now as I was still slowly sipping my first.

Ahmet and Mustafa generously offered us to eat from their table and poured us both a glass of *raki*. As Ahmet proceeded to add water to our glasses, Mandy stopped him and said she would drink hers straight. Ahmet laughed.

"It's too strong to drink straight," I advised. "It's meant to be drank with water and ice and enjoyed slowly whilst you graze from the *meze*."

"I like my spirits straight," Mandy replied.

"Zoe is correct. *Raki* is a very strong drink," said Ahmet.

He was amused and translated the situation to his friend who smiled and shook his head.

"Oh, you guys haven't seen me drink," boasted Mandy. "I can drink any of you under the table. Just you watch."

"But Mandy, really this drink is very strong," I warned as she downed her first glass of *raki*.

She didn't seem to even hear me as she offered up her glass for more.

I knew now what everyone had been talking about. She had a serious drink problem. I felt out of my league as there was no way of controlling her or curbing her drinking.

The conversation flowed and I enjoyed my glass of *raki,* sipping it slowly. I washed it down with some of the white cheeses and yoghurt as is the traditional way. The *raki* table is an important aspect of Turkish culture. It is always served with a range of appetisers and the focus is on conversation and friendship. It isn't a drink to be gulped down quickly but try telling that to Mandy.

I started to notice that she didn't look so good.

"Are you ok?" I asked.

Mandy just sat there frozen. She was as still as a statue. Her face was white. She was gazing aimlessly into the distance and beads of sweat were visible on her brow and under her eyes. This had happened so suddenly. One minute she was chatting away and downing *raki* shots and now nothing, silence.

"Mandy," I asked again. "How are you feeling?"

She mumbled something undecipherable.

"Mandy?"

"I can't move," she slurred. "I don't feel good."

I tried to help her out of her chair but she was a dead weight. Ahmet offered to help me carry her to the bathroom. This was a disaster. Never again, I was thinking. We got her to the bathroom just in time but it wasn't pretty. Now what should I do? I needed to get her home. I was feeling angry and annoyed. We had all told her about the potency of *raki* and yet after three pints of beer, she still insisted on drinking the *raki* straight.

Mustafa had his car there but it was against all my safety codes to get into a stranger's car. However at the time, it did seem the easiest option. We managed to load Mandy into the back seat and within minutes she threw up again all over his car. I was horrified. The look on Mustafa's face said it all.

"Where does she live?" asked Ahmet.

Their afternoon had now been spoilt and I felt terrible. I also realised that I had no idea where Mandy lived.

"Oh, I don't know." I replied apologetically. "Just let me call one of the other teachers that she lives with."

Mandy was now slumped over in the back seat of Mustafa's car and mumbling to herself. She was a complete mess and the car stank from her vomit. I was so embarrassed by her behaviour. I didn't know how we could ever repay these guys for their kindness and help.

"Hello Louis. This is Zoe."

Luckily for me, Louis had answered his phone almost immediately.

"Hello Zoe. How are you?" asked Louis.

Over the past weeks, Louis and I had become quite good friends and we had shared a few lunches together. I was well aware of his thoughts and opinions on Mandy but as he was her flatmate, I had to call him. I didn't know what else to do.

"Well Louis, I'm really sorry to bother you but I have a bit of a situation here and I need your help," I asked.

"Sure, what's up?" he replied.

"I went out for a drink with Mandy and now she is so drunk, paralytic in fact. I'm so angry with her. Anyway, now I need to get her home but I don't know where you guys live. A kind gentleman here has offered to drive us but I need your address. Also, would you be able to meet me down on the street to help me carry her home. She's a dead weight." I asked.

"No, no, no. I'm done with carrying her home. She's not a child. I'm sorry Zoe, but she's not my problem. She's not yours either." he retorted.

He told me the address and hung up. Understandably he was not amused and in no mood to deal with a drunk Mandy again.

Thanks to these two chivalrous Turkish gentlemen, I managed to get Mandy home. Louis was furious when he opened the door and I totally understood now what they had been talking about. She was a disaster and this was just the first of many such encounters I was to have with Mandy.

From that day on, Mandy looked to me as an ally and I never had the heart to ignore her or turn my back on her, but she did cause me a lot of grief at times. It wasn't uncommon for her to call me in the middle of the night because she was drunk and didn't know where she was. Of course, all I could do was instruct her to hail a taxi.

On other occasions, she would ring my door bell in the early hours of the morning. She wouldn't stop ringing it until I let her in and then she would sit in my kitchen and cry her eyes out about her children. Really a very sad person and my first ever experience with an alcoholic.

Chapter Thirty One

I still received an occasional phone call from Murat. When he called it was always the same story of woe and misery and to be quite honest, I was over it. It was his culture so he knew better than me what was expected of him. I understood that he needed to keep the family happy and his bosses happy and that meant staying married to Asli. Of course, I felt for him as he was torn between what was his duty and what he really wanted to do, which was to be with me.

"If I leave her to be with you, will you stay with me for always?" he would ask. "Or will you go back to Australia?"

For him it seemed to be a big gamble. Understandably, he didn't want to end up alone. His sons had threatened to disown him but he was sure that in time they would come back to him. The rest of his family would also disown him and he would be ostracised from any future family occasions. He didn't mind that too much as long as he was with me.

"Murat, I can't guarantee anything. Life is not like that," I would reply. "I think you need to try and make your marriage work."

I certainly didn't want any responsibility for his decisions and I seriously couldn't see a long term future together. Since moving to Turkey I had witnessed another side to his personality and I hadn't liked it. He had tried to control me and impose his Turkish macho beliefs on me. He didn't like me going out with friends. He didn't like that I was finding my way without him.

It was best that we made a break now and I was happy to throw myself into my work. In such a short time, my school life had gone from strength to strength. I was feeling much more confident as a teacher and I felt loved and appreciated by my students. My social life was soaring and I was making many new friendships.

My evening classes finished at ten o'clock and then it was normal to go out for a drink with some of the other teachers. Sometimes it was just a hot chocolate at Café Dunyasi, downstairs and other times we would go to a café or bar for a few alcoholic beverages.

On the weekend evenings we would go to the nightclub where we had spent New Year's Eve and dance the night away. I loved this place for its 'Turkishness'. It was dark and dingy, smoke filled and the music was loud. Turkish rock mostly but sometimes an American rock anthem would be attempted to be sung. As I said before, if a fire ever broke out, this place would have been a death trap as the only exit was a narrow stairwell to safety but to date no such disaster had occurred, thankfully.

Sometimes the teachers organised an afternoon at the ten pin bowling alley. I hadn't been bowling for years and had forgotten how much fun it was. I don't think I had felt this happy or laughed so much in years. I definitely was enjoying my new life in Turkey and I guess I will always have Murat to thank for that. If it hadn't been for him, would I have ever thought to come to Turkey or embark on such an amazing adventure?

The terrace at our school was a great social meeting place. We had a ten minute break after every lesson and I would always go up to the terrace and mingle with my students. They had been so welcoming from the very first day and I felt I had built a strong rapport with most of them. Getting to know them out of class gave me an insight into their family lives and valuable lessons about Turkish culture.

For example, one of my students, Ezgi was a bright and intelligent twenty eight year old woman. Her English was very good and we could often have some rather in-depth conversations about life in general. She had a brilliant mop of golden copper hair, quite unusual for a Turkish woman. She told me that her father had been Bulgarian and perhaps that's where it had originated from. Her father had passed away a few years before and now she lived at home with her mother and her older sister. Both she and her older sister were unmarried. This was rather late in the Turkish scheme of things. Her sister had wanted desperately to marry but so far no suitors had come her way.

Ezgi, on the other hand, did not want to marry. She wanted a career. She had already studied fashion at university but no longer enjoyed that scene. She had recently applied to Turkish Airlines for a stewardess position. She had secretly travelled to Istanbul for the interview and having been successful, she was now expected to move to Antalya for training.

Proudly she announced this news to her family. She fully expected their congratulations and blessings in her new career move. Instead, she received a serious scolding from both her mother and her sister. Her mother had told her that if she accepted this job as a 'cheap waitress on an airline', she would disown her. I was beginning to realise that this 'disowning threat' is apparently a common punishment in Turkey.

Ezgi was broken and down hearted. I tried to explain that a stewardess on Turkish Airlines would be a wonderful career and that she should be so proud of herself for succeeding. Furthermore, a mother's love can never be broken and that probably her mother was just scared of her moving away. I could see how torn Ezgi was over this. It was unfathomable to me that a mother could threaten such a thing. I had a lot to learn about Turkish culture and how they viewed different aspects of life. That's the difference between living in a country and just visiting on holiday. When you live in the country you are able to delve deeper into the culture and see the reality. After much agonising over the career that she had dreamed of, Ezgi decided against the move to Antalya and remained at her mother's side as the loyal and faithful daughter.

Another young student had come to me with another more shocking concern. I felt honoured that she felt she could confide me but I was totally out of my depth with this one. In conservative Turkish society young women must be virgins at the time of their marriage. Her boyfriend was impatient and not prepared to wait. To maintain her virginity he insisted on her submitting to anal sex. She obliged but understandably felt used and even ashamed. She wanted it to stop but didn't want to lose her boyfriend. I could only comfort her with the advice that she should only do what she wanted to do and never feel pressured to take part in an activity that she clearly didn't enjoy or want.

Living in Turkey, even just a couple of months was allowing me to get below the surface, to see the layers that one never sees on a short holiday. Turkey was perplexing to me. On one hand things seemed quite modern and yet on the other hand, it still held on tightly to old traditions and beliefs that seemed so out of place in the twenty first century. The Turkish youth were trying to find their way but still the constraints of societal beliefs and parental control influenced their every move.

Since moving to Turkey, one thing that had always made me gasp and take a step back was the very visible military presence. Never in my life had I experienced seeing so many soldiers and police armed with very serious looking guns and rifles. At the time in 2009, there had been many protests in the streets against Israel, condemning Israel's actions against the Palestinians in the Gaza War. I had never seen protests of this magnitude before.

The riot police had lined the streets and were a very imposing and chilling sight. They were armed and held huge transparent polycarbonate shields in front of them. The protesters had marched down the main street holding placards and chanting their protests in Turkish. Fortunately, I never saw any violence and though very loud, these protests seemed to pass by peacefully.

One day at school our terrace was completely taken over by the military. It was surreal to say the least. Across

230

the road in a park, many important and high ranking Turkish officials were meeting for some sort of military ceremony and therefore our terrace was the scene of military snipers to watch over the event.

To see these soldiers up close was daunting with their massive sniper guns aimed out over the street. After the initial shock at tea time, we relaxed a little and accepted the situation. It was after all, not something you see at school every day. Many of my students managed to get photos of these soldiers who were quite obliging and happy to be snapped.

On another occasion the Prime Minister of Turkey, Recep Tayyip Erdoğan was coming to town to campaign for an upcoming election. The venue for the campaign was a huge car park that was used for the weekly markets. Another teacher and I were curious to see what went on and so we braved the cold weather and went along. The entire area was a mass of blue and gold flags for the ruling Justice and Development Party better known as the AK party. Massive red and white Turkish flags hung from surrounding buildings as well as gigantic posters of Erdoğan and Atatürk. There were many vendors selling flags and other AK Party merchandise. The massive crowd was throbbing and there was high excitement as they awaited the arrival of their Prime Minister.

On the centre stage was another larger than life picture of Mustafa Kemel Atatürk, the founder of the Republic of

Turkey. Military style band music was blaring out of loudspeakers and the patriotic crowd was getting more and more pumped. As we looked around we saw heavily armed soldier above shops and buildings watching down on us and the street activities. Apparently people's homes had been commandeered so that the soldiers could take over their balconies or living rooms, where ever they had the best view. The noise, the colour and the excitement; this was something I had never ever experienced before. This was Turkey.

Chapter Thirty Two

During one particular lesson, we were reading from our textbooks. Unfortunately, I hadn't read ahead and therefore wasn't prepared for what was to be a sad and very upsetting fifty minutes.

The chapter was about natural disasters. There were short passages to read about the various types of natural disasters that had, throughout history, caused havoc on the planet by their destruction and loss of life. At the time, I had thought it an interesting chapter. Generally, the students disliked their textbook and I had to agree that some of the stories and activities were quite dull and boring. But this chapter I thought with its pictures and statistics was more interesting and the following questions would motivate the students to converse. I clearly wasn't thinking.

I read out the first question to the class.

"Has anyone experienced a natural disaster?"

The hands went up and everyone was keen to talk and tell me their story. At first I thought that this was a positive sign and that I had motivated my students more than I had thought. I soon realised that I had hit upon a tremendously sensitive subject and that the pain of their memories was still vivid and fresh.

"My teacher, do you know that on August 17, 1999 we had an earthquake here in Izmit?" asked Bulent. "It was very big and destroyed our city and homes and many people died."

"Oh Bulent, I'm very sorry. I remember now," I apologised but it was too late.

The floodgates had been opened and I listened as my students recalled that fateful morning. Most of them had been teenagers or even younger when this catastrophe had hit. The epicentre had been some ten kilometres from the centre of Izmit city and it took just thirty seven seconds for thousands of lives to be lost and hundreds of thousands of people to become homeless. The most damage was done in the surrounding towns and villages. Even Istanbul, seventy kilometres away, suffered considerable damage.

Each student had their memories and their stories to share with me. It was heart-breaking. Some had lost family members. Most had lost their homes. The city and surrounds had been in chaos. It had been the height of summer. The daytime temperatures had been in the high thirties and the bodies were decaying fast. The local ice skating rink had been turned into a temporary morgue and family members could search there for the bodies of their loved ones. For the many thousands of injured, make shift medical tents were set up to provide much needed treatment. Conditions weren't ideal for amputations and other serious injuries but it was the best that they could do.

Medical support and rescue teams from around the world had come to offer their services. For days they pulled bodies from the rubble and spirits were lifted with the miraculous stories of survivors being found alive days after the event.

One student described how he and his sister were whisked away to family on the Black Sea. They had stayed there for two years whilst their mother and father tried to rebuild their home. The tears were running down his cheeks as he described his feelings of loss and how much he missed his mother.

Other students had similar stories to tell. They wanted to tell their story. It was ten years ago but the pain was still visible and the memories were still fresh.

Another student explained to me what he had experienced. It had been a very warm night and he and his cousin had been sitting outside down near the seafront. The moon was big and bright and there was a strange glow. They had witnessed waves forming on a normally peaceful sea and ran to get their parents. They knew that something was not right. As the earthquake struck, their home like many others crumbled to the ground but they and their parents' lives had been spared.

I was relieved when finally the buzzer announced break time. My class were still processing their thoughts and the mood was very sombre. I encouraged them to go up to the terrace for some fresh air and a tea. I was saddened by their stories and couldn't imagine what emotional turmoil they had undergone over the last ten years. There had endured the fear, the terror, the pain of losing family members, losing their homes and the abandonment they felt when they were sent away to safer places whilst their parents rebuilt.

I put that chapter of the textbook to bed and opened the next lesson with some word games that always brought a smile to my students' faces.

"Change seats if you are wearing glasses," I called.

Sixteen chairs and seventeen people including me. This game was loud and sometimes quite dangerous as everyone jostled for a chair; a version of musical chairs that tested their language skills and understanding. The person left without a chair then stood in front of the class and it was their turn to make the next suggestion.

"Change seats if you are wearing jeans."

"Change seats if you like chocolate."

This game never failed to please and was a classroom favourite. As my teaching skills improved, I began to learn many English focused games that added fun and variety to my classes. Certainly after our intense first lesson, these students needed a good laugh.

Chapter Thirty Three

During my skype interview for this teaching job back in Australia, we had of course, discussed all the benefits. The pay rate they offered at that time was certainly more than enough to live a comfortable life in Turkey. As they were desperate to get native speakers, the package that they had offered was very attractive.

Pay was always in cash. We were paid monthly on the fifteenth of every month. On pay day we would go to the office and receive a white envelope with our name on it. Inside would be a short handwritten tab with our hours worked and the amount paid. Sometimes I would receive the amount of four thousand Turkish liras, all in five lira notes. It did all seem a bit shady but the pay was good so no one was complaining. There was no way I could spend that sort of money in a month and I had a healthy wad of Turkish lira hidden in my suitcase. As the months went by, the thickness of that money envelope just grew and grew. It felt like Monopoly money.

"Just get some money out of the suitcase," I'd say to Matt.

We certainly didn't have a lot of furniture but we didn't hold back on eating, drinking and travelling. We did whatever we wanted and still had money left over. For example, a *döner kebab* was two lira. A nice meal at a good restaurant was maybe twenty lira a head. It was impossible for us to spend four thousand lira in a month.

On top of a very healthy cash payment, the school also paid a housing allowance. That was a contribution towards renting our own flat. If you wished to stay living in the staff housing after three months, you didn't receive the housing allowance but I would say all the teachers had their own flats and received the healthy housing allowance too.

Another incentive was that the school would arrange the teachers' work visas. With a tourist visa one can only stay in Turkey for ninety days and also, it was illegal to work on a tourist visa. Back in 2009 it was still possible to do a visa run. Many of the schools in Istanbul would get a small bus and take their teachers over the Bulgarian border for the day and then return with a new ninety day stamp in their passports.

My school did one better. They offered to arrange residency and my work visas. It all sounded good. So before my ninety day tourist visa expired, plans were underway to arrange for my residency. It soon became apparent that this too was on the shady side.

First step was that one of the office workers would accompany me to a Turkish bank. She didn't speak English and I didn't speak Turkish but she knew what she had to do, and I soon got the idea. At the time, it was estimated that four thousand American dollars was the necessary amount for living costs for twelve months in Turkey. Therefore, one had to have proof of being able to support oneself for twelve months before they could get a residency visa. So a bank account was opened in my name and a deposit of four thousand American dollars was made into my account by my school.

Next, the necessary paperwork from the bank showing my healthy bank balance was taken to the appropriate government office for foreigners' residency. Lots of waiting and paperwork followed. The office girl then stated that I was a family friend that had come to stay with her family to experience life in Turkey. I found this all out later. I was asked some questions which, of course, I couldn't answer as I didn't understand the questions. The official behind the counter eyed me up and down with a sceptical glint in his eye as he forcefully stamped my papers. I had to submit three passport size photos and in three weeks' time I could come and pick up my official *'Yabancilara Mahsus Ikamet Tezkeresi'* or Residence Permit for Foreigners. It was that easy.

Then we returned to the bank. We withdrew the four thousand American dollars and closed the account. As I said, all a bit shady but as I was told again and again; this is Turkey. When I picked up my *'Ikamet'* I was very proud of the small blue book with my photo inside. It allowed me residency for twelve months. The only problem I could see now was that it clearly stated inside the cover of my *'Ikamet'* that it was illegal to work on this visa. Would we ever get work visas?

Talking with the other teachers, it became apparent that we had all gone through the same process and we were all now in possession of the same residency visa. No one had a work visa. This was slightly unnerving because we had heard stories of teachers in Istanbul being forcibly removed from class and subsequently deported for working illegally on a tourist visa.

It was not uncommon for the police to do 'surprise' raids on language schools in the effort to uncover illegal workers. Well, not so much of a surprise really. One morning all of the foreign teachers received a text message from Karen instructing us not to come in to school until further notice. Only the Turkish English teachers were on duty when the police made an 'impromptu' visit to our school. There had obviously been a tip off. Later that day we all received text messages that evening classes would resume as normal.

Not only had management texted us all to stay home that morning but they had also removed all our class role books and folders. It was obvious that this wasn't the first time that this had happened as they were all well versed in the procedure. I later found out that it was all just a formality really. The police knew the school employed foreign teachers. They knew that they didn't have work visas and they just turned a blind eye to this. In fact, many of the police even came to English lessons or sent their kids there. Turkey just had a way of making everything work and for the least cost. Getting work visas for sixteen foreign teachers would have cost quite a small fortune, so naturally they didn't want to go to the expense and trouble of doing so. Looking at it from the employer's perspective too, they could go to the work and expense and then have the teacher prematurely leave as with what happened with Angie.

This ability to turn a blind eye to things was a very Turkish trait that I would never have experienced in Australia. I witnessed it many ways. If someone at the supermarket didn't have enough money to pay for their purchases, the teller would just wave them off. In Australia, the teller would definitely insist on every last cent. I saw people board the bus without enough bus fare and again the driver would just wave them on. It was a very charitable approach to life and I admired that about the Turkish people. They cared about those less fortunate than themselves.

Another incentive my school offered was an end of contract payment. It was quite a nice amount in American dollars that they would pay if you finished a twelve month contract. I didn't stay the entire twelve months but I did receive half the payment for six months which I thought was very generous.

Despite the slightly unconventional and generally illegal doings of the school, it was in the end trying to better the lives of its citizens. Being able to speak English was a powerful tool in landing a lucrative and fulfilling job and I was a crucial part of that process. It did feel rewarding.

Chapter Thirty Four

Those first two months had flown by and finally it was time for Matt to board the plane for Istanbul. I was beside myself and couldn't wait to see him again. My students were also eagerly awaiting him. I had, of course, told them of his imminent arrival and they were more than keen to include him in their activities and show him around their city. He would be quite a celebrity.

The day of his arrival I jumped on the morning bus into Istanbul to meet him at the airport. There would certainly be many occasions when we could explore Istanbul together but I knew that at this time, he would be jetlagged and very tired. It was best to bring him straight home. He would certainly laugh at our new living arrangements but it was, after all, only for a short time.

I really only thought about spending the year in Turkey. We would maybe set off on some travels in July and return home to Australia in the latter part of the year. As for my flat, I was quite sure that we would be moving on by the summer so for the next few months it was adequate. It was an adventure. It was like luxury camping.

"So when are you moving in?" asked Matt with a grin as he walked in the front door and had a brief look around.

I had expected some sort of smart comment. I just laughed.

"You have a bed, we have a table and two chairs and there is a very efficient heating system and a fully functioning bathroom. What more do you need?" I replied.

"And because you are a boy, I gave you the blue room." I laughed. "I even bought you blue curtains."

Matt just laughed at the paint job in our new home. Paint speckles over the newly laid floor boards and every room a different but bright colour. The enormous salon or living room was painted a lovely canary yellow and was completely empty.

"This can be our exercise room," I suggested. "We have plenty of room to run around."

Matt ventured out onto the balcony and checked out our location. Huge neon signs lit up the road and the park. In the distance we could see snow topped mountains.

"Good central location," he remarked.

"Yes. And my language school is just over there," I pointed. "About a three minute walk away. I'll take you there tomorrow. Everyone is very keen to meet you."

I was very eager to show Matt around Izmit and show him my new way of living. As a family we had done some lengthy travels around Australia and Europe. But we had also taken the boys to more exotic locations such as Thailand, Bali and Morocco, so I knew that it was highly unlikely that Matt would experience any kind of culture shock.

It had always been my intention and desire to show my children as much of this amazing world as possible. We had visited the hill tribes in Thailand and he had seen how people had lived in small grass huts. We had seen people bathing and washing their clothes as we floated down along the Mekong River to Myanmar. We had spent a month travelling Morocco and ventured off the beaten track into the Atlas and Rif mountains and Sahara desert. So I was confident that Matt would easily adjust to Turkish life. I had no concerns there. However, when you travel to a foreign country, especially one that is so different to our own, there are customs and ways that one needs to adjust to.

The next day I was working the afternoon shift and therefore after a good long sleep, Matt was welcome to accompany me to school. First, I took him to the staff room and introduced him to any teachers that were there. He got to meet Dianne. Then I took him to Karen's office and she was really thrilled to meet him and welcomed him warmly to the academy. She was more than happy for him to come to my classes whenever he wished. Matt was a very likeable kid and thankfully everyone was very welcoming.

Since I had left Matt in Australia, he had let his hair grow and had a couple of piercings. He also sported a little growth on his chin, not quite a beard but still rather cute. Karen had commented that he would be quite a hit with the girls and he was.

That first evening he came to my class and I soon realised that as well travelled as he was, I hadn't prepared him for greetings in Turkey. The first to come forward was a favourite student of mine called Mert.

Mert was into heavy metal music and always dressed in black. He also had long hair and lots of piercings in his ears and eyebrows. I was always drawn to Mert because of his deep and insightful comments in class. He was always willing to offer an opinion and that made for good conversation. I also saw him as a good friend for Matt.

That first meeting was so funny. Seeing Matt as he entered my classroom, Mert sprang up from his seat to greet him. As is usual in Turkish culture, Mert extended his hand to Matt and leaned in to kiss him on the cheeks. Matt instantly pulled away. Bless him, Mert tried again. Again Matt pulled away. He just wasn't sure what was going on. We were all laughing at this stage.

"Matt, it's customary to greet with a kiss on each cheek or at least to touch cheeks," I explained through my laughter. "Even guys greet that way."

All the class was laughing by now as they realised how Matt had been taken off guard by this foreign custom.

"It doesn't take long for it to all seem quite normal and everyone is kissing everyone at every meeting," I explained.

It's true that the Turkish people are a very touchy-feely race of people. It's not unusual for male students to sit during class with their arms around each other or even rest their head on their friend's shoulder. They are not necessarily gay. It's just part of the culture. The girls will always walk along holding hands or arms linked. They feel quite comfortable playing with each other's hair or cuddling up in class. They are a very warm and affectionate people. If I met any of my students out of class we would always greet with kisses and a hug. It was just normal. There was warmth and a closeness that I would never have experienced in Australia. We, in the west have lost that connection with our fellow man and find it strange at first.

On the other hand, something else I noticed in Turkey was the lack of personal space. In Australia we are very used to a large area around ourselves. Australia is a ginormous country with a relatively small population so we are spoilt in terms of space. Whether we were talking, queuing, picnicking or relaxing on the beach, we would always try to be as far away from the next person as was possible. Here in Turkey, I noticed that the people like to be close. Even if there were many free seats on the bus or ferry, a Turkish person would still choose to sit next to another person. Sometimes that would infuriate me. I'd look around and see all the empty seats. So why has this woman choose to sit so close to me? Later, when we went for picnics, I realised that we would set up our grill next to another party's grill; safety in number perhaps, a sense of security and something that they are used to. I guess that is all part of living and experiencing a new culture.

Even before class had officially started, Matt was surrounded by his new friends. Everyone was so welcoming and happy for him to be a part of our class. I thought it best that everyone sit down and we could do some formal introductions.

"Good evening class. Hope everyone is well. He's finally here. This is my son Matt," I announced. "Maybe we can go around the class and you can each introduce yourself and then if you like, you can ask Matt some questions. Is that OK with you, Matt?"

"Sure." I could see that Matt was feeling his celebrity status at this time and he was slightly overwhelmed with all the attention. The introductions began.

"*Merhaba* Matt. I'm *Fatma*."

"*Merhaba* Matt. I'm *Emre*."

As each student announced their name, Matt nodded, smiled and replied with a 'Hi'. I knew he couldn't possibly remember everyone's name but it was a good ice breaker. He was enjoying his new position in my class and it was all going so well. Then it all fell apart.

"*Merhaba* Matt. My name is *Fatih*."

Now '*Fatih*' is a popular Turkish name and is pronounced as 'farty'. Matt just couldn't keep a straight face and as he returned the greeting he exploded into laughter. Typical school boy humour. I tried to keep my composure. Of course, I knew what he was laughing about but my students did not. They had absolutely no idea at what was so funny. I had tried ever so hard to stay serious. Finally, I totally lost control too. I was laughing at Matt. His laughter was contagious. Tears were streaming down

250

my cheeks. There was Matt and I bent over with laughter and my sixteen students looking on in bewilderment. I'm sure they were thinking that these Australians are a strange breed.

I had another student in a later class called *Ufuk*. I was dreading the introductions. Even I always tried to refrain from using his name as I knew I would say it wrong. So this time I prepared Matt. I pleaded with him to keep a serious face and be respectful and luckily we got through that without teacher and son breaking down in hilarity.

Chapter Thirty Five

As the year progressed, Matt and I were both enjoying our time in Izmit. Even our day to day life was an adventure. Really, you never knew what the day would bring.

One thing very noticeable in Izmit at this time was the number of gypsies on the streets begging for money. If you sat at an outdoor café enjoying a beverage, inevitably before not too long, you would be approached for money. Initially, we would give our small change until we were warned not to do so.

"Don't give them money," said Louis one day. "They are just con artists and that is their business."

"Really?" I replied in disbelief. "But some of them look so poor and some are even disabled or have sick children.

I saw one guy sitting on the ground in the park and he had no legs. "

"It's all a con. Believe me," he continued. "They keep their children home from school to beg and as long as you keep giving them money, they will keep keeping the kids home from school. The guy with no legs is being exploited by his family. How do you think he gets to the park?"

That all made sense but still I couldn't believe that anyone would make their children appear sick, just so that they could beg for money. The thought of family members setting this poor legless guy up in the park so that he can beg was repulsive. In Istanbul with Murat, I had witnessed little children standing in the middle of four busy lanes of traffic trying to sell bottles of water to the motorists.

"My God, that is so dangerous," I had said to Murat. "They can easily be hit by a car."

Murat had basically said the same as Louis.

"As long as we continue to buy the bottles of water from these children, their parents will continue to keep them home from school and make them stand out in the busy traffic."

It was a hard lesson to learn and it did take me a while.

As we didn't have a washing machine in our flat, it was a weekly trip to the laundromat. It was about a ten minute walk away up the main street of Izmit. Matt and I would each carry a bag full of dirty washing and we would leave it there and pick it up a few hours later, all clean and folded. On our usual route up the main thoroughfare, we often passed a gypsy woman sitting in a doorway with a sickly child laid across her lap. She would rock forward, mumbling something in Turkish and put her hands out for money. Matt and I didn't have the heart to refuse her a small donation. We couldn't be as heartless as Louis and Murat.

This one particular day we passed this poor woman on our way and left her a few coins as we continued on to the laundromat. She always smiled and nodded back to us. It wasn't much but we felt we had made a contribution to her survival. Maybe it was for the days' food or perhaps it went towards her son's medical treatment.

At the laundromat, we were invited by the owner to stay a while and enjoy a glass of tea with her and her daughter. It was my day off and we had nowhere in particular to be and so we happily accepted her offer. There was the obvious language barrier but we still managed to communicate and have a few laughs. After many teas and possibly an hour or so later, it was time for us to be on our way and we would return later in the day to collect our washing.

As we once again approached the 'poor' gypsy woman, there she was with her young son, both sitting happily on the doorstep eating ice cream. The young lad didn't look so sickly now and as we passed her by, she just shot us a cheeky smile. Yes, we had been conned…..many times….Louis had been right. We could only laugh and realise that another lesson had been learnt; don't give money to the beggars.

But I was a slow learner. On another occasion, I was walking home from work when I was approached by a young woman in colourful gypsy clothes. She spoke to me in Turkish with a sad and pathetic expression. She continued to gesture with her hand to her mouth and rubbing her stomach. Her face expressed pure desperation. I didn't know what to do. I'd been told not to give money to the beggars and I had learnt my lesson the hard way with the ice cream licking gypsy woman but this young woman was obviously hungry.

"Hmm, what should I do?" I thought to myself.

She didn't let up and kept following me. She wanted money and saw me as an easy target, I'm sure. Then I had an idea. I wouldn't give her money. I would take her into the kebab shop and buy her a kebab. I motioned for her to come with me into the kebab shop but she insisted on putting her hand out for money. I was ready to walk away and continue my path home.

She grabbed my arm and nodded that she would accept a kebab instead of the money. We entered the kebab shop and I let her order from the menu. A kebab was, at this time, two lira. She ordered and I felt happy and confident that I had helped her and I happily gave her the two lira to pay the man. As soon as those liras touched her palm, she was off up the street as fast as lightening. Again I had been tricked.

"Hey, Matt. I'm home. Look what I've got for you? Just picked you up a kebab on the way home."

"Thanks mum," he replied.

Of course, he was in stitches when I told him the account of my latest conning incident.

"You are so gullible, mum," he said with a grin as he devoured his kebab.

Another time I was sitting outside at the tables of Starbucks enjoying a coffee and going through my lesson plan. Along came a guy pushing a cart laden high with the most beautiful deep dark black cherries. I had to have some. I approached the guy and asked their cost. He showed me ten fingers and so considering the cost of cherries in Australia, I thought that ten liras for a kilo of these beauties was reasonable.

Sitting back at the table now, one of my students soon joined me.

"Oh, *kirazlar*. You like?" she asked.

"Yes, Matt and I love cherries. They are one of my favourite fruits," I replied.

"Yes, very delicious," she said. "I want too."

The guy with his cart was fifty or so metres down the street now. She quickly left her seat and ran after him, coming back with her own bag of cherries.

"Five liras a kilo is too much," she exclaimed. "Still they are best quality."

"Five liras?" I cried. "That bastard. He charged me ten liras."

Again, I had been tricked. All I could do was laugh. They were so clever at it and so skilled. They could easily pick the '*yabanci*', the foreigner and we were easy prey. In the end, I reasoned a few liras here and there, wasn't going to break me and I guess they really needed it.

The worst con and definitely the most costly that I experienced was when Matt and I decided to give up our flat and go travelling. I'd worked for almost seven months and it was time to do some exploring together. I had given my notice in at work and I had also let my landlord know that we were moving on. As is normal I didn't pay the last month's rent as I had been a month in advance. Turning off all the utilities was the last job. The two young ladies from school accompanied me to the offices and I received my deposits back for the water and the electricity.

I still needed to turn off the gas. I tried to contact the student whose name I had opened the account in. He was not answering his phone.

"Karen, do you have any other contact details for the student, Irfan whose name my gas account is in?" I asked.

"Ah no, same number as you. Leave it with me. I'll get the girls to call him," she replied.

They had no luck either. In fact, Irfan had stopped coming to classes. I was beginning to get concerned now. It was, after all, close to a three hundred lira deposit. That's quite a bit of money and was the largest of the deposits.

"So I want to close my gas, but we can't seem to contact Irfan," I explained to Louis as we were enjoying a coffee at our local Starbucks.

"Did you tell Karen to get on to it?" asked Louis.

"Yes. They have called and I have called numerous times but his phone just rings out," I replied.

"Hmm, here," said Louis. "Use my phone."

What a clever idea, I thought. I dialled Irfan's number with Louis's phone and it rang as usual. The caller ID would show that it was Louis calling.

"*Efendim*," he answered.

"Hi Irfan, its Zoe," I replied.

Suddenly, the phone went dead.

"He hung up on me," I exclaimed.

"Hmm, you've been had, Zoe," explained Louis, shaking his head. "He has no intention of giving you back the deposit. He'll close the account in his own good time and walk away with your three hundred lira."

I couldn't believe it. I couldn't believe that people could do something like that. I was so naïve. These people were obviously desperate and they saw all of us foreigners as wealthy. They had no qualms about cheating and tricking us. I was really pissed off. My school continued to try and locate Irfan but he was never heard of again. Another lesson learnt.

Chapter Thirty Six

Over those first few months, Matt was having quite an active social life. In the beginning he came to most of my evening classes but usually skipped the morning ones. I would go off to work and leave him sleeping peacefully at home. Sometimes he would meet me after class and we would venture down to the sea front and enjoy a long and leisurely lunch in one of the restaurants there. If it was a sunny day, it was just so pleasant to sit outside and enjoy lunch and a beer or two with the warmth of the sun on our backs.

Sitting gazing out to the sea we would watch the many navy boats patrolling the area. It was always exciting when we saw a submarine glide by. As there was a major military base in a neighbouring town of Gölcük, there was often plenty of naval action out to sea. There was also an awesome military museum that we had visited and I had my first time inside a submarine. I can say that I was very happy when I finally managed to crawl out. It was so tight and claustrophobic and I couldn't imagine how men could stay under the sea for up to three months.

Matt had his social life with me, often coming out with all the teachers from school. We had our dance nights and our ten pin bowling evenings. He also had his own set of friends that he liked to hang out with. He and Mert had become great mates and they would often go into Istanbul to see a concert or visit Mert's favourite heavy metal bar in Taksim. He was only eighteen years old and although I worried all the time, I had to let him go and trust that he would always be sensible.

Another group of his friends that were all my students would often go out on picnics. One of the guys, Bulent had a car and so they could go to Lake Sapanci or to the nearby snow fields up at Kartepe. That was where Murat and I had planned to go on that fateful day. Matt was having an awesome time and I was so happy that he had adjusted and made friends so easily. What became evident to me on the times I had also accompanied them on a picnic, was how they could find happiness and fun in the simplest of ways. These guys were all university students in their early twenties and they still enjoyed skipping rope and playing chase. There was still a childlike wonder that percolated through their activities and even their conversations. I felt quite confident that Matt was in safe hands.

As the weather started to improve and spring was in the air, Matt and I made frequent trips to Istanbul to explore all the major tourist attractions. Of course, we wandered all the popular sights in the Sultanahmet area. From the *Kapalıçarşı* also known as the Grand Bazaar to the amazing underground Basilica Cistern, to the spectacular Blue Mosque and the Aya Sofia, we explored them all.

We liked to take the ferry boat to Ortaköy, a popular neighbourhood of Istanbul on the shores of the Bosphorus and below the iconic Bosphorus Bridge. Sitting on the outer deck of the ferry, we enjoyed the fresh crisp sea air and the views of the spectacular seafront houses from the Ottoman times.

On arriving in Ortaköy, we always made our way straight to the row of little stalls sitting along a cobbled stoned pedestrian lane and selling one of Turkey's most delicious fast food treats; *kumpir*. Yes, you can get this tasty street food elsewhere, but everyone knows that an *Ortaköy kumpir* is the best and it certainly was one of our favourite treats.

Kumpir is simply a baked potato. But what makes it so special is the multitude of fillings that are piled and squashed into the centre of the potato. The potato is taken from the oven, split open and the insides are mashed with butter and cheese and then you select what fillings you want stuffed inside. Matt's eyes were always bigger than his stomach. I could never finish mine as it was just so big but we sure did love our *kumpir*.

We enjoyed many colourful days in Istanbul and we had become quite familiar with many of the neighbourhoods. We knew our way around, the best places to eat and the best sights to see.

One weekend I was working and Mandy was not. Unbelievably, besides arriving at Istanbul's airport, she had never yet been into the city. She wanted to make a day trip and knowing how familiar we now were in Istanbul, she asked if Matt would accompany her and show her around. I was definitely a bit sceptical at first but then thought to myself what could possibly go wrong. It was daytime. I was confident that Matt was always sensible and always acted responsibly. He could show her around and take her to the main attractions. Matt was fine with the idea as he had nothing else on.

They took the morning bus to Harem and then the ferry across to Eminönü which is close to the heart of Sultanahmet and all the main attractions. Well, my poor Matt. Of course, I called him throughout the day to see how they were going. From the ferry boat, Mandy had insisted that she was thirsty and their first stop of the day was to a bar where Mandy had her first beer of the day.

According to Matt, she had no interest in seeing the sights and was only interested in having a few beers and flirting with the men in the carpet shop. In fact, she had set up a date with one of the carpet sellers and Matt was furious. I felt terrible that I had agreed to this venture and put him in such a difficult situation.

It was not long before it was quite apparent that Mandy was completely inebriated and Matt was left with the task of getting her home. What a disaster of a day. What sort of person could do that to a young eighteen year old? An alcoholic, of course. I guess both Matt and I were still a bit naïve and too trusting. Of course, he could have left her with her new carpet shop boyfriend but he did his best to get her on the ferry home and Mandy could set up her date for another day. That totally ended my friendship with Mandy and I no longer felt any sense of pity for her. She had abused my trust. She was a walking disaster.

By now, I had received my Turkish Residency visa which was valid for twelve months from the date of issue. However, Matt only had a ninety day visa and his time was almost up. We needed to do a visa run. He needed to get a new stamp in his passport for another ninety days. We thought about our options. We could simply do the more popular bus trip over the Bulgarian border. That was the easiest and the least costly but we had heard about long queues and lengthy waits at the border. It didn't sound too appealing.

"This is our year of adventure. Let's do something really exciting. Let's go to Petra," I suggested.

"Yeah cool," replied Matt. "Hmm, mum, where's Petra?"

"Jordan," I laughed. "Petra is a UNESCO world heritage site. It's an ancient city in the desert and I have always wanted to go there."

"Well let's do it," said Matt.

Karen was most accommodating with giving me some extra time off work. After all, I had at that time been working well over forty hours a week. The pay was nice and I had quite a healthy wad of notes in my suitcase now. We just needed to book some flights and a few days later we were jetting off to Amman.

The entire Jordan trip was amazing. Travelling with my son was the most awesome experience. I felt so blessed to have this special time with him and to create such colourful memories. We visited all the main tourist attractions but our day hiking in Petra was a definite highlight as was 4WDing through the Wadi Rum in the footsteps of Lawrence of Arabia.

We returned to Turkey with a new visa in Matt's passport and a strong yearning to do more travels. We had tasted adventure and now we were hungry for more.

The whole Turkish coastline and south east was beckoning us and we began to plot our route.

Chapter Thirty Seven

Coming to Izmit to teach English had been an incredible journey. I had stepped right out of my comfort zone. I had left my comfortable home in Australia to come to the great unknown. I had proved to myself that I still had plenty of life left in me. Being in my fifties wasn't a barrier to living the life that I wanted. For me personally, it had been a life changing event and I knew that my life would never be quite the same again. I couldn't go back to my unhappy existence in Australia. I was sure now that I wanted a divorce.

If Steve and I had nothing in common before, well now that chasm had got even deeper. I felt like I had rediscovered the 'old' me. I had travelled extensively before meeting Steve and having my family. Back then I had embraced everything that life had to offer. And then somehow, as the years went by, I lost myself. I didn't know who I was if I wasn't a wife and mother. But now, I was back. The 'old' Zoe was back. That spark had been rekindled, reawakened. I could see an exciting future and a world of possibilities.

My son Matt had joined me on this path and we had shared so many unforgettable moments together. I had witnessed Matt grow and shine before me. He had easily assimilated into his new environment. He had made so many new friends and enjoyed many new experiences. He was even speaking better Turkish than me. He had learnt the joys of living minimal. Yes, we joked about it all the time, but let's face it; we don't really need so many material objects in our life. We were on an adventure and surely this was part of the deal. We had a roof over our heads and we were comfortable enough. Thinking back to our home in Australia set on five acres in the countryside and with our own swimming pool, we knew we were privileged but we also knew that we were adaptable. We had developed a genuine fondness for our Turkish home; the squeaky elevator that struggled to make it to the fourth floor, our kind and generous neighbour who often brought us Turkish treats. It had been an enlightening few months and we had both grown as people and if it was at all possible, Matt and I were closer than ever. I didn't want that to end.

"Karen, I'm really sorry, but I want to give you my notice," I said. 'It's been a learning experience and I'm so grateful that you gave me this opportunity but I want to go travelling with my son now," I explained. "Our recent trip to Jordan has whetted our appetites and now we want more. We want to explore more of Turkey."

Karen understood. She was a mother too. To have this special time with our children is precious and we all know that the day is coming when they will prefer to go travelling with their friends. So I was going to grab this last opportunity to spend quality time with Matt and further explore this diverse and vibrant country.

As for Murat, I had fewer and fewer calls and messages from him. It was for the best. He had resigned himself to the fact that he was tied to Asli and leaving her would only bring him more and more pain. He would have lost his family and most importantly the love of his sons.

Murat had been a part of my memories from my twenties and now he was a part of my memories in my fifties. I couldn't deny that his love had brought me out of a deep dark hole of helplessness and set me afloat on this new path. I would always be grateful to him for that. Still I couldn't have guaranteed him a life together and I certainly didn't want to be the reason he lost his sons. Even though Murat seemed at times to possess western thinking, the cultural differences had become ever so obvious and I know that for both of us it would have become intolerable. I wouldn't have been able to deal with his domineering behaviour and he wouldn't have been able to accept that I was a strong, capable and independent woman. For both of us it was just a fleeting moment of happiness when we both could forget our problems at home. The reality was that we both needed to face those problems before we could truly move on.

As Murat's and my relationship had sizzled out well before Matt's arrival, there had been no need for introductions and no need for me to even mention anything about Murat to Matt. It was best that way. I was, after all, always a mother first. Sadly, I didn't have any more contact with Nihal either, as the language barrier prevented us from having any discussions on the matter anyway. I still received an occasional 'hello' text from Meryem but basically those friendships were collateral damage from our breakup.

Over the next month, Matt and I went about the motions of giving away our few house hold items. There was nothing to sell really. I had organised one of my students to come and pick up everything with his cousin's truck. He would take the mattresses to his parent's home in the village. Matt and I had busily researched and plotted out our journey. It was thrilling to think that we were about to embark on a new adventure. For me, my time in Izmit had been remarkable and life changing. I had found my calling as an English teacher and I knew that I would return to teaching later. For Matt it had been a period of growth and change. We had both made many warm and sincere friendships and it was quite sad to be saying goodbye, but we planned on seeing some of these friends again later.

Our great mate Mert had been called up to do his military service and was being sent to a military base in Diyarbakir in the south east of Turkey. We had promised him that we would put Diyarbakir on our travel itinerary and definitely come and spend a day with him.

As we boarded the bus for Izmir, we were once again stepping into the unknown and excited for what lay ahead. A new chapter of our Turkish adventure was about to begin. The thrill of travel was beckoning us to explore all the exotic corners of this diverse and beautiful country. Who knew what we would discover and who we would meet along the way?

Beyond that, Matt had university back in Sydney and for me.....well, who knows?

THE END

ABOUT THE AUTHOR

Matilda Voss is a fifty something solo traveller, English teacher and expat currently living in Spain.

She was born in England but spent most of her life in Australia before taking the plunge and moving to Turkey to teach English. Though she only meant to stay a year, she ended up living there for six years.

Matilda loves to travel and has visited close to fifty countries. She loves experiencing new cultures and Turkey will always hold a special place in her heart. She has travelled extensively throughout Turkey from border to border and her experiences are the inspirations for her stories.

She has a travel blog where she writes about her journeys and hopes to inspire other women over fifty to get out on the road and explore this beautiful planet. She truly believes that age is just a number.

www.womansolo.com

If you would like to contact Matilda she promises to answer all emails.

Best wishes.

Matilda   Matildavoss@gmail.com